Taken by surprise . . .

Fargo awoke with a start. He looked over at Heather, who still lay by the campfire. From his position he could take down anyone who came after her—her voice would be a surefire alarm if ever there was one—but there was no one else in sight.

He had no idea how long he'd been asleep, and Heather hadn't made a sound.

So why had he awakened so suddenly?

The answer came as something hard and cold pressed into the side of his neck. Fargo blinked, taking a second to identify the touch against his neck: the muzzle of a six-gun. The man's voice came next, no whisper, and with almost an admiring tone to it.

"Not bad, mister. It would have worked with most," the voice said. "But then again, I ain't most."

Fargo heard the hammer click back—it was the sound of his own death. . . .

THE TRAILSMAN

#229

MANITOBA MARAUDERS

by

Jon Sharpe

A SIGNET BOOK

SIGNET
Published by New American Library, a division of
Penguin Putnam Inc., 375 Hudson Street,
New York, New York 10014, U.S.A.
Penguin Books Ltd, 27 Wrights Lane,
London W8 5TZ, England
Penguin Books Australia Ltd,
Ringwood, Victoria, Australia
Penguin Books Canada Ltd, 10 Alcorn Avenue,
Toronto, Ontario, Canada M4V 3B2
Penguin Books (N.Z.) Ltd, 182–190 Wairau Road,
Auckland 10, New Zealand

Penguin Books Ltd, Registered Offices:
Harmondsworth, Middlesex, England

First published by Signet, an imprint of New American Library,
a division of Penguin Putnam Inc.

First Printing, November 2000
10 9 8 7 6 5 4 3 2 1

The first chapter of this book originally appeared in *Wyoming War Cry*,
the two hundred twenty-eighth volume in this series.

Ⓟ REGISTERED TRADEMARK—MARCA REGISTRADA

Printed in the United States of America

PUBLISHER'S NOTE
This is a work of fiction. Names, characters, places, and incidents either are
the product of the author's imagination or are used fictitiously, and any
resemblance to actual persons, living or dead, business establishments,
events, or locales is entirely coincidental.

BOOKS ARE AVAILABLE AT QUANTITY DISCOUNTS WHEN USED TO PROMOTE PRODUCTS
OR SERVICES. FOR INFORMATION PLEASE WRITE TO PREMIUM MARKETING DIVISION,
PENGUIN PUTNAM INC., 375 HUDSON STREET, NEW YORK, NEW YORK 10014.

The Trailsman

Beginnings . . . they bend the tree and they mark the man. Skye Fargo was born when he was eighteen. Terror was his midwife, vengeance his first cry. Killing spawned Skye Fargo, ruthless, cold-blooded murder. Out of the acrid smoke of gunpowder still hanging in the air, he rose, cried out a promise never forgotten.

The Trailsman they began to call him all across the West: searcher, scout, hunter, the man who could see where others only looked, his skills for hire but not his soul, the man who lived each day to the fullest, yet trailed each to-morrow. Skye Fargo, the Trailsman, and the seeker who could take the wildness of a land and the wanting of a woman and make them his own.

1861—in the northwest provinces of the giant called Canada. A new land brings new dangers unlike any faced before, where sometimes the choice between compassion and killing is no choice at all. . . .

1

The big man riding the magnificent Ovaro let his lips thin in a tight line. Habit was a terrible burden he swore, an unfair taskmaster, pushing you to do things you wanted to ignore. It made today captive of yesterday. Regardless, his lake-blue eyes stayed narrowed as he watched the young woman nose her horse through a narrow passageway of jack pine and paper birch. He stayed in his own nest of pine as his eyes shifted to the six horsemen that followed her. They had split into two groups of three each, one trio staying behind the young woman, the other increasing speed to outflank her in the trees. Skye Fargo drew a deep breath and cursed habit again as he moved closer, cutting his own way through the thick woods.

This was not his land. He was a visitor here, a sightseer, a vacationer. He'd come wanting to see the land, to feel the majesty of it, and ride the beauty of it. He'd already seen how it had its own character, a magnificence at once awesomely beautiful and frightening. He had the feeling that here, in this vast land called Canada, beauty and richness existed as a temporary gift from the great fierceness of the northland. But trouble was trouble. It always had its own marks and wore its own signs. Skye Fargo knew those signs, and also knew that they were the same all over. They were why he sat in the pines and watched the six riders as they closed in on the young woman. Old habits refused to leave a man alone.

It had all begun in the little town of Lakeshore, in the small hotel near the west shore of Lake Winnipeg. Fargo had taken a room there, stabling the Ovaro and then sitting down to a drink of good Canadian whiskey and a meal of jack pine savage venison roast. Six men were in a wooden booth just to one side of him, their voices carrying clearly. With a quick glance, he stole a fast look at them. All wore worn, raggedy outfits and all had the hard, tight faces of men who lived their lives scrounging at the bottom of the barrel. He'd seen their kind often enough back in the states.

"It's got to be her," a man with a red-and-black checked shirt said. He had a long nose and a pinched face that gave him a weasel-like appearance. "She fits the description," he continued. "They figured she'd be coming this way and looky here, she's all alone boys."

"Then we do it," one of the others said in a gravelly voice. "If we make a mistake, so what?" he added callously.

Fargo looked away as he took another sip of his drink. "We wait for her at the end of town?" one of the others asked.

"Two of us watch there come morning. Two of us stay here in case she's at the hotel. Two of us cover up and down main street," the one with the long nose said. "When we spot her, we follow her and find the right spot near the lake, where we can dump her."

"Not before we have ourselves a taste of her," the gravelly-voiced one said.

"You got a one-track mind, Joey," the other snickered.

"You all want some too. I just say it," Joey's raspy voice answered. In agreement the group fell silent as they finished their meal. Fargo's venison roast came as they were leaving, and Fargo remembered telling himself it was none of his damned business. Here, he was a stranger in a strange land, determined to enjoy himself. He certainly hadn't come all the way up here to find trouble. Somebody else could see to it, he told himself and put it out of his mind as he attacked his venison. But by the time he finished his meal he was cursing old habits again. A young woman was going to die. He knew she would be beaten and violated by those animals, and then they would kill her. He'd never been able to turn his back on someone in trouble. He'd paid his bill and gone to his second-floor hotel room. A single bed and a dresser with a big pitcher of water waited for him there. It was all he needed, he thought as he undressed, fitting his long frame onto the bed as best he could. He went to sleep knowing he didn't need to wrestle with making decisions. The past had already made them for him.

He'd set the inner alarm clock he'd learned to use and dressed before daybreak. He went to the stable, retrieved the Ovaro and wedged himself between two shacks that let him see the hotel. Two of the six men arrived and took up positions of their own, both near the hotel. The watching game had begun. Over an hour passed before the streets filled with wagons and riders. Eventually, the girl came out of the hotel.

Fargo glanced at one of the two men, saw him signal to the other and returned his eyes to the young woman. She wore a floppy, wide-brimmed hat that hid most of her face but he saw a well-formed figure, a brown vest over a tan shirt, Levis encasing slender legs, a neat, contained figure with what seemed to be modest breasts. She went around to the stable behind the hotel, finally emerging riding a dapple-grey gelding.

She rode down the main street, not hurrying, and the two men immediately fell in behind her, keeping their distance. Fargo moved from his vantage place, hung far back, and soon saw the first two men joined by the rest of the gang. The young woman rode away from town, staying along the wide road. Finally, she turned into the thick pine forests that spread out on both sides of the road. She rode up an incline that leveled off after about thirty yards. Fargo watched the men follow. He turned the Ovaro into a thick line of trees and moved closer as he saw the two groups of men speed up to close in on the young woman. She rode idly, pausing to admire flowers and trees, obviously simply enjoying herself. The riders split up into two groups, one set moved faster while the other trio hung back. Fargo kept pace with the first three and watched them surprise the young woman as they pushed out of the trees in front of her. Fargo took note that the long-nosed one led the troop.

"Heather Grandy?" the man asked.

"Who's asking?" the young woman said, her head lifting high enough to allow Fargo to see under the wide-brimmed, floppy hat. He took in a soft-lined

4

face, quietly lovely, with wide, hazel eyes, full, red lips and a firm chin.

"You don't need to know that," the long-nosed one said.

"Then you don't need an answer," the girl returned.

"Don't be like that, honey. We came all this way to give you a good time," the man said, and one of the others snickered. As he watched, Fargo saw the young woman reach down and come up with a riding crop in her hand.

"Now what do you figure to do with that?" long-nose said chidingly. The young woman's arm snapped out with the speed of a lightning bolt, slashing the riding crop across the man's face. "Ow, Jesus!" he screamed as a line of red erupted on his face. He twisted in the saddle, lost his balance, and fell from his horse. The girl spun her dapple-grey and put the mount into an instant gallop, racing away.

Her reaction had been so viciously swift that she might have made her escape. Unfortunately for her, she ran head-on into the second trio, which had come up behind her. With their guns drawn, they blocked her way and she reluctantly reined to a halt. "End of the road, honey," the gravel-voiced one said. "Drop it," he ordered, gesturing toward the riding crop. The young woman let the crop fall from her hand as the three men came forward, one taking hold of her mount's cheek strap. They led her back to where the long-nosed one still pressed a kerchief to his face. He rose from one knee and started for the girl.

"Kill her, goddammit," he snarled as the other

three pulled the girl from her horse. He started to rush at her, but the others held him back.

"Easy, Bert," one said. "No sense in wasting a good thing."

"Bastards," the young woman spit out at her captors. She whirled around and tried to rake her nails across the face of the nearest man. He managed to twist away as one of the others slammed a fist into the girl's kidney from behind her. She gasped in pain and pitched forward onto her hands and knees. One of the others grabbed her arms and flipped her onto her back as a third one fell on top of her. He straddled her and began to tear her shirt open.

"Let's see what you got, honey." He laughed as the girl twisted helplessly. Fargo grimaced, the big Henry already out of its saddle case. He raised the rifle and fired. The one on top of her screamed in pain as the bullet shattered his shoulder blade. He fell off the girl and Fargo fired again. The one holding her arms flew backwards, both hands clutching at his abdomen. Fargo saw the other four, six-guns in hand, peering into the trees as they searched for their attackers. The girl had smartly rolled herself into a ball and lay still. Fargo slid silently from the saddle. He knew the four men would zero in on his voice, or his next shot. They'd send bullets spraying and he didn't want the Ovaro hit by their wild volleys. He left the horse, moved a half-dozen yards away and flattened himself on the ground beside the trunk of a big jack pine with the silence of a cougar on the prowl.

He peered out at the four men. They were frozen in place, watching for a movement, listening for any sound. Fargo saw the beads of perspiration rolling down their faces and decided to stay silent. They were already near the breaking point, small-time thugs with neither the experience, the training nor the inner steel to control their nerves. He let the seconds tick off, watching as the one with the slash across his face licked the dryness from his lips. He continued to stay silent as he saw the mounting nervousness seize the four men. With his rifle at his shoulder, Fargo remained beside the tree, almost smiling as he saw one of the four swallow hard, his hands trembling. It hadn't been much more than thirty seconds before one of them finally broke. It was the long-nosed one, but instead of making a move against his attacker, he caught Fargo by surprise by diving at the girl and making a shield out of her.

Fargo swung the big Henry, followed the diving figure and fired. The shot exploded just as the man reached the curled-up figure. Pitching forward, the diving figure landed half over the girl with a last shuddering gasp of breath. Fargo saw her uncurl and use her legs to kick the limp figure away from her. The other three fired a volley of shots into the trees. They sprayed the area and their bullets thudded into the trunk of the tree where Fargo hid. He stayed where he was, anticipating their next move. He heard their footsteps as they started to run away and he rolled out from behind the tree, watching them run to their horses. They were leaping into their saddles as Fargo rose on one knee, fired, and smiled as one of the trio flew from his horse. But the other two were racing away. Fargo rose, ran and vaulted onto the Ovaro.

He swerved the pinto between two pines and galloped after the fleeing riders, quickly glimpsing them

7

as they tried to steer their horses through the dense forest. But their horses were as ordinary as they were and they had to slow down as they maneuvered their way through the denseness of the pines. The Ovaro, using its powerful, jet-black hindquarters to cut in and out without losing any speed, closed the distance in minutes. Fargo raised the rifle to his shoulder again, took a moment to aim, waited for a clear shot, and fired, two shots echoing almost as one. Both the riders made strange, jerking motions as they fell from their horses and vanished in the brush. Fargo slowed the pinto, moved forward carefully and found both figures motionless in the high grass. He slowly turned the pinto around.

He made his way back to where the attack had begun and found the young woman on her feet, bending over one of the lifeless forms. She looked up as he appeared and swung down from the Ovaro. "I was going through their pockets, thought they might have something to identify them," she said with more calmness than he expected.

"Did they?" he asked, and she shook her head. She had taken off her hat, and he saw very deep, rich auburn hair that gave a new beauty to her face. The tan shirt tightened as she rose and he decided her breasts were perhaps not as modest as he'd first thought. "Whoever they were, they were definitely after you," Fargo said.

"How do you know that?" she asked.

"Overheard them talking last night. They had a description of you and an idea you'd be heading this way. They planned to get you. That's why I'm here," Fargo explained.

She stepped forward, extended a hand and he felt a

firm grip. "Most would have gone their own way," she said.

"Thought about it," he smiled. "Couldn't shake off old habits."

"Thank God for that," she said. "You're an American."

"Bull's-eye."

"You got a name?"

"Fargo.... Skye Fargo. In the States, some call me the Trailsman." Her eyes widened.

"Really? It's a strange world. I've been looking for someone who can uncover a trail for me. In fact I've already spoken to a few men about the job," she said.

"Are you Heather Grandy?" Fargo queried.

"Yes," she said and ran one hand through the deep-auburn hair. "I wonder why they were after me?"

"None of my business," Fargo shrugged.

"It will be if I hired you, Fargo." Heather Grandy smiled.

"I'm not here to work. I'm having myself a vacation," Fargo said. "I've never seen this part of your country."

"I'll make it more than worthwhile to skip your vacation," the young woman said, and her hand closed around his arm. "We have to talk more. How about tomorrow? I'm meeting with someone this afternoon."

"If it's somebody you're meeting for the job, I'd say hire him," Fargo remarked.

"No, it's a man whom I just met. He took a real fancy to me," Heather Grandy said.

"Can't blame him for that," Fargo said.

"Gallantry in word as well as deed. You're an unusual man, Fargo," she said. "Please think about letting me hire you?"

"I'll think about it, but no promises." He smiled, and suddenly her lips were on his, very soft and moist. Her kiss was a steady pressure that combined both pleasure and promise.

"That's to help you think," she murmured. "And for everything you did just now." When she pulled back, her hazel eyes had grown darker, a soft, simmering quality in their depths. She turned and pulled herself onto the dapple-grey. "I'm staying in the hotel in Lakeshore," she said. "I'll wait there for you." He watched her ride away with a great deal more composure than most young women would have displayed after barely avoiding a vicious attack. He waited until she was out of sight before climbing onto the pinto, passing the figures on the ground. Someone would find them sooner or later he thought as he moved on.

He was glad he'd followed old habits but he had certainly had his fill. He wanted to continue his vacation although he had to admit to himself that she was a very attractive young woman. Exploring this land with her might add another meaning to the word vacation. Still, all he wanted to do was to simply relax. He had broken trail for a large herd of Holsteins all the way from Kansas to Jim Mannion in upper Minnesota. He'd decided to go exploring the prairie province known as Rupert's Land, later called Manitoba.

Now he slowly continued his trip, taking in the feel of the land with its vast network of lakes and rivers. In some ways, it was not that different from the States, and in other ways, it had its own, special character. Even the names had their own feel to them, Dog Lake, Jackhead, Crane River, Reindeer Island, Dauphin, Neepawa, Wicked Point and so many others. They echoed the heritage of the land and nodded to the fierceness of the great Canadian winters. He had already seen moose and reindeer, but he knew the vast herds were still far to the north. It was summer and for the first time he felt like he was on vacation as he rode through vast fields of scarlet butterfly weed, wild bergamot, blue flag iris and purple loco, forests of white pine, jack pine, northern white cedar and juniper. The relaxed pleasures of the day began to draw to a close as he made his way back along the shore of Lake Winnipeg. He was nearing the hotel when he glimpsed Heather Grandy walking beside a slightly portly man in a tan frock coat and well-tailored trousers. Fargo saw a heavy face with thick, black hair and a flashy ring on one hand. He also saw the bulge of a holster under the frock coat.

As Heather walked on down the street with the man, Fargo rode the pinto to the stable, returned to the hotel and had a leisurely meal. He paused at the desk and asked the clerk about Heather Grandy, finding out she had the room adjoining his. After a nightcap of one more smooth Canadian whiskey, he retired to his room, his body telling him he had ridden farther than he realized. He undressed, and idly made plans for moving northward via one of the flatboats that plied Lake Winnipeg. Finally, sleep wrapped itself around him and the little room grew silent.

He guessed a few hours had passed, when sounds woke him. He pushed up on one elbow, and heard a man's voice raised in anger coming from the room next to him. A woman's voice answered and he instantly recognized it as Heather's, muffled as it was. He couldn't make out words but there was a sharpness in her tone. The man's voice came again, louder, demanding, then came noises that sounded like a scuffle. Fargo had just swung his long legs over the edge of the narrow bed when he heard a single, popping sound, not really loud, not unlike the sound of a cork being pulled from a wine bottle. But it wasn't a cork. He knew that sound. It was the unmistakable sound of a derringer going off. He frowned into the dark, frozen for a moment, and then another sound exploded, loud and deep. This was the instantly recognizable sound of a big-bore revolver.

Leaping from his bed, he pulled on trousers and strapped on his gun belt as he dashed from the room. He was at the door of the adjoining room in seconds, turning the knob and swinging the door wide open. He burst in, Colt in hand. Heather Grandy turned as he came in, her eyes wide; she was looking lovely in an emerald-green dress with a deep V neckline. He tore his eyes from the soft swell of her cleavage, and brought them to the figure on the floor. It was the man he had seen with her earlier in the day, only now he was lying on his back, very dead, with a circular stain spreading across his silk shirt. Fargo saw the revolver on the floor, a big .44-caliber Remington Army revolver with an eight-inch barrel. Heather flew to him and wrapped her arms around him.

"He was going to rape me," she gasped. "He was starting to do it and he wouldn't stop." Fargo half turned at the sound behind him. The desk clerk stood in the doorway, staring down at the lifeless figure.

"My God," he breathed. "I'm getting the sheriff." Spinning, he raced away down the hall. Fargo turned back to Heather Grandy as she clung to his arm.

"He pinned me on the bed. He wouldn't listen to me, wouldn't stop," she said. "I saw the gun and pulled it from his holster. He grabbed at it and we fought. It was either that or let him rape me, and I wasn't about to do that." She halted, peered at Fargo. "Where were you? How'd you get here so fast?" she asked.

"In the next room," he said and she leaned her head on his chest.

"It seems you know when I need you. I'm glad for that," Heather murmured, and he felt the soft swell of her breasts against him. He held her but his eyes narrowed in thought. He had no reason not to accept the story as she told it to him. It was a chain of events that happened all the time, an unfortunate pattern in the relationships of some men and women. But she hadn't told him all of it. The sound of the derringer stuck in his mind. She hadn't mentioned that, and he frowned. He wasn't one for imagining sounds. He was about to ask her about it when he heard footsteps coming down the hall. Heather stepped back as the desk clerk entered with a man wearing a sheriff's badge and another with a deputy's shield. The sheriff, a square-faced man with salt-and-pepper hair, stared down at the man on the floor.

"Ernie Binder," he grunted.

"You know him?" Heather said.

"Local gambler. Big man with dice and dames," the sheriff said. "I'm Sheriff Greavy."

"Heather Grandy. I've been staying here at the hotel," Heather said.

"You kill him?" Sheriff Greavy asked.

"I'm afraid so. I had to," Heather replied.

"You want to fill me in?" the sheriff said.

"I met him a few days ago. He was very attentive. We spent the evening dining and drinking, but when he brought me back here he tried to force himself on me. I didn't expect that," Heather said.

"You that innocent?" the sheriff tossed at her.

Fargo saw her hazel eyes flare. "I guess so," she snapped and proceeded to tell the sheriff the details she had told Fargo. When she finished, the sheriff pursed his lips.

"It's not a new story. You just made it turn out differently than it usually does," he said.

"I'd rather my way than his," Heather said.

"I don't disbelieve you, but it's just your word. He's not talking," the sheriff said. "I like something more than just somebody's word."

"How about common sense, the look of things, logic?" Heather returned. "I told you what happened. I grabbed his gun to defend myself. I don't carry a big six-gun."

The sheriff knelt down to the man and searched through his pockets, drawing out some change and a few pound notes. "Ernie always carried a big roll of American dollars, at least a thousand if not more. He called it his 'on-the-spot bankroll.' It's not here," Greavy said.

"Are you saying I robbed him?" Heather frowned.

"Feel free to search my things. I shot him to stop him from raping me. That's what it was, nothing else."

The sheriff turned to Fargo. "Who are you and where do you fit in here, mister?" he asked.

"Name's Skye Fargo. I'm in the room next door. I heard the noise, then the shot, and came to see," Fargo said.

"Really now? Way I see it, you could've shot him, over her, maybe. I want more than words," Greavy said.

"Seems that's what you'll have to go with, hers and mine," Fargo said.

"Not completely," the sheriff said and turned to the desk clerk. "Get Doc Hawthorn," he said, and the clerk hurried away. He ran to the salon next door and returned minutes later with a tall, thin man carrying a black doctor's bag. He wore horn-rimmed glasses that sat on a thin, straight nose. Fargo instantly smelled the scent of alcohol on him. The doctor glanced down at the man on the floor.

"Ernie Binder?" he said.

"Himself," Greavy grunted. "We'll take him to your place. You'll get me something besides words, something like a bullet." He turned to Fargo. "You're carrying a Colt. If the bullet the doc takes out of Ernie Binder is from a Colt, you're in trouble, mister. If it's a forty-four caliber from a Remington, you're in the clear. So's the lady. It'll back up her story on using his own gun on him."

"Fair enough," Fargo said. As the sheriff's deputy and the desk clerk carried Ernie Binder from the room, Sheriff Greavy turned to Heather.

"Stay in the hotel till we get back to you," he said.

15

"Same for you, Fargo." He strode from the room and Fargo met Heather's eyes.

"Thanks for being here," she said. "I knew it wouldn't go easily. Sheriffs never take a woman's word on its own."

"I'll get dressed," Fargo said. "It could be a long wait."

"I hope the doctor finds the bullet. We're both in trouble if he doesn't," Heather said.

"Why wouldn't he?" Fargo questioned.

"I don't know." Heather shrugged. "Maybe it's not in him. Maybe it went clear through him."

"Then it ought to be on the floor here someplace. Let's have a look," Fargo said and started to move slowly across one side of the room. Heather took the other side and joined him as he ended his search peering under the bed. No bullet turned up. Fargo pushed to his feet. "Guess we wait for what the doc finds," he said. "I'll see you later."

He turned and walked to the door, saw her watching him. She had the same calm manner as she had after the six men tried to attack her. He wondered if it was self-discipline or part of her nature. Whichever it was, not many young women had it, he commented silently. Reaching his room, he closed the door, dressed, and stretched out on the bed. He found himself frowning into space as his thoughts kept returning to the sound of the derringer. Heather hadn't mentioned a derringer to the sheriff, either. Yet he was sure he had heard the sound of the gun, Fargo told himself as his lips thinned. Could he be certain of what he'd heard? The question danced in his mind. It had happened moments after he'd wakened. Had he heard something else? Dammit, he swore angrily. The

16

derringer made a distinctive sound and he didn't go for imagining things. His lips stayed tight as he swore to himself he'd find out the truth. It had become a question he'd not carry around with him unanswered, he decided as he closed his eyes to wait. Either way it was quite clear to him that his vacation was over.

2

The wait wasn't as long as Fargo had expected, and he soon heard the sheriff's voice call his name from down the hall. He rose, went out to see the lawman entering Heather's room and followed him in. "Doc Hawthorn got the bullet out," the sheriff said. "It's a forty-four slug from a Remington. That lets you off the hook, Fargo. Same for you, Miss Grandy. There's nothing to contradict your explanation of what happened. . . . Fact is, it follows what other women have said about Ernie Binder. I can go with self-defense."

"Thank you, Sheriff. That's what it was," Heather said.

"I'm still wondering about the bankroll Ernie always carried," Greavy said.

"I'm afraid I don't know anything about that, but you're still welcome to search my things," Heather said.

"Don't figure I'll find anything," Greavy said and Fargo smiled inwardly. The sheriff had his own streak of practical wisdom. "You staying long in town?" Greavy asked, turning to him.

"Expect I'll be leaving tomorrow," Fargo said.

"And you?" the sheriff asked of Heather.

"Probably tomorrow," she replied, and Greavy uttered a satisfied grunt, nodded and walked out of the room. Heather stepped to Fargo.

"We have to talk in the morning," she said.

"Count on it," Fargo said and hurried out of the room. He walked from the hotel, went down the dark street outside, and found the doctor's large, white house. He saw a light on, and after a few moments the doctor answered his knock. He was still wearing a blood-streaked apron, his shirt sleeves rolled up, and he held a glass of whiskey in one hand.

"What are you doing here?" The man frowned, his words slurred.

"Came to see you," Fargo said. "Want you to look for a bullet."

"I found the bullet," the doctor said.

"Another bullet," Fargo said.

"There was only one bullet, mister," the doc said, annoyance coming into his voice.

"Maybe not," Fargo said.

"The desk clerk heard only one shot. One shot, one bullet. Go home, mister," the doc said and took a pull on his drink. He slammed the door shut and Fargo frowned. The desk clerk was too far away to have heard anything but the loud report of the Remington. But was that really the only sound? The question still speared at him. But the doctor wasn't about to help him, he knew. Fargo backed from the house as the light went out. He waited and watched, and soon a low lamplight came on in another room of the house. He followed, peering through the window and seeing the doc finishing his glass of whiskey.

After the man drained his drink, he pulled off his clothes and fell onto a bed, lying still. The house grew silent, but the body of Ernie Binder lay somewhere inside it, most likely in the room where the doc had done his probing. It would stay there, probably packed with ice around it, until they came to remove it the next day. Fargo left the window and crept to another, found it locked and went on to the next. He tried three windows until he found an open one and crawled into the house. Inside, he saw a candle giving off a dim glow at the end of a hallway and he followed the corridor to a closed door where the odor of formaldehyde was an unmistakable signpost. Carefully sliding the door open, the smell instantly grew stronger, and he peered into the darkness. He saw the outlined shape of a lamp on a table. He made his way to it, turned it on, and closed the door. The lamplight spread and illuminated the long table and the sheet draped over the form atop it.

Fargo stepped to the table and saw the bags of ice packed around the body. Drawing back the sheet, he stared at Ernie Binder, a series of bandages across the center of his chest. Alongside the table, Fargo saw a small tray holding various surgical instruments. He picked up a scissorslike tool and first cut off the crisscrossed bandages. Then, using the same instrument, he began to probe into the opened incision in the man's chest. Working slowly, feeling his way with the instrument, he found the man's heart, a ragged half circle inside it. The ragged hole made it clear that he'd found where the doc had cut into the man's heart and found the bullet.

Probing carefully, Fargo moved the instrument up and down, then sideways, then in a circle, inching his way inside the corpse's chest cavity. He nudged tendons, muscles, veins, ligaments, and bones. He pressed aside cartilage, poked at ribs, scraped along

20

the right edge of the sternum, touching, feeling, pausing as his hands grew red. But suddenly he halted. The instrument had touched something deep at the back of the chest, something not of tissue, muscle or bone—a hard, unyielding object. He opened the tool wider, carefully maneuvered it around the edges of the object and pulled. It came out at once and he drew the instrument out of the body. Fargo stared down at the small metal object in his hand. Wiping the blood from it, he saw it was a twenty-two caliber shell from a derringer.

It bore marks where it had struck a rib. He saw a basin of water nearby and immersed the shell in it until it was free of blood. Leaving the instrument in the basin, he picked up the shell with his fingers. He let out a grunt of satisfaction, knowing that he hadn't imagined hearing the derringer's shot. Drying the small slug, he put it in his pocket and realized little beads of perspiration had formed on his brow. Probing inside a body was neither something familiar to him nor his idea of a good time. He put the bandages back in place across Ernie Binder's chest and quietly stole back along the hall. He reached the window and climbed out.

Once outside, he returned to the hotel, went to his room, and slept the few hours left until morning. When he woke, he washed, dressed and then went to Heather's room. She answered at his knock, looking quite fetching in a yellow shirt and black slacks, her hazel eyes holding little glints inside them. "Been waiting for you. Been storing up things to talk to you about," Heather said.

"I've something myself," Fargo said evenly and tossed the little slug on the bed. Heather stared at it for a long moment, her face expressionless. "Little something I retrieved," Fargo said.

Heather's eyes went to him, the edge of a wry little smile pulling on her lovely lips. "I'm impressed," she murmured. "How did you know?"

"I know the sound of a derringer when I hear one," Fargo said.

Heather's smile widened. "You were in the next room and heard it," she said, and he nodded. "You had to go to a lot of trouble to get that shell. Why?" she asked.

"I don't like games. You didn't tell me and you didn't tell the sheriff," Fargo said. "But you killed him with your derringer, then shot him with his Remington. Why?"

"I had to. I pulled my derringer but he wouldn't stop. He laughed at me, lunged at me, and I fired. After I shot him I knew they'd never believe my story if they knew I'd used my derringer. Hell, you saw how suspicious Greavy was."

"True enough," Fargo agreed.

"I took his gun and shot him with it because I knew it'd make a better story, one they could believe. Turned out I was right," Heather said.

Fargo let her explanation turn inside him. She was right about the Sheriff. Greavy wouldn't have accepted the self-defense excuse if there'd been no sign of a struggle. Still, Heather had done some damn fast thinking. Perhaps too fast. He was still turning the question over in his mind when she slid her arms around his neck.

"Nothing's changed. I had to defend myself. I just made it so they'd believe me," she said, holding him.

"You held out telling me, too," Fargo commented.

"I was suddenly afraid maybe you wouldn't believe me, either," Heather said. "I decided it was best not to say anything to anybody. It didn't quite work with you and I'm glad for that."

"Glad?" he echoed.

"Yes. It proves you're special. I said I'd like to hire you. Now I'm certain. I need someone like you."

"What'd you do with your derringer?" Fargo queried.

"Threw it out the window, just in case they decided to search," Heather said. "I want to hire you, Fargo. I want you to help me. I'll pay real well, a thousand dollars up front, another thousand when you finish."

He let a low whistle escape his lips. "A lot of money."

"I want the best," she said. Fargo's eyes moved across her deep auburn hair, the hazel eyes, and full lips. She was almost too lovely not to believe, and he had no real reason not to accept her explanations. They were understandable, reasonable. He just couldn't stop wondering if she was really just fast thinking or terribly clever. But he'd no question about one thing. She was intriguing and he was drawn to her, to say nothing of the kind of money only a fool would turn down. Besides, it'd be a new experience to take a vacation and get paid at the same time. She moved and he felt the tips of her breasts brush against his chest.

"Maybe you'd best spell out the details," he said.

"Is that a yes?" Heather asked, excitement alighting on her voice.

"Guess so," he nodded and her kiss was warm and quick.

"Then let's get started. I'll meet you at the stable," she said.

"What about your derringer?" he asked.

"I'll get it before I meet you," she said. He nodded, then went to his room and gathered his things. He had the Ovaro saddled when she came along. She had changed into Levis and a yellow sweater that showed the high roundness of her bosom. He swung in beside her as she rode from the stable on her dapple-grey.

"You get your derringer?" he asked.

"No. Somebody must have found it," she said and put her horse into a trot. "We'll ride north to Lake Winnipeg, take the flatboat there and keep on going north."

"How far north?"

"We may get close to Port Nelson. That's far enough north for me. The southern end of the timberline starts there," she said.

"Meaning no trees north of the timberline."

"Hardly any. The timberline runs in an uneven path into the Northwest Territories. It's all mostly frozen tundra from there."

"I came to explore Manitoba. It seems I'll be having my own, personal guide," Fargo said as they rode from town.

"Everybody calls the province Manitoba, but the name isn't official, don't expect it will be for another eight years. The name comes from the Indian name *Manitou*, Great Spirit. Meanwhile, like most all of Canada, this is Hudson Bay Company land. They own and run most everything ever since King Charles the Second chartered it all to them in sixteen seventy. There are other companies that operate here, but Hudson Bay is the powerhouse. You could say

Canada and Hudson Bay have been one and the same since old Charles the Second. Things are changing, but it'll take time for a new government to form," Heather said as she led the way over slightly swampy ground, past towns named Dog Lake, Moosehorn, Deep Rock and Little Saskatchewan.

"I'm still waiting for details. Where are we going and why?"

"I guess you could say I'm going home. I sure won't be welcomed by everybody though," she said with a chuckle.

"Why's that?" Fargo inquired.

"Past differences," she answered.

"Why go, then?" he pressed.

"Things I have to attend to, starting with my father. I've gotten word that he may be in real trouble. He may even be dead. I want to find out," Heather said. "My father is the founder of Grandy Export Company. We're in the same business as the Hudson Bay Company, only we're small fish compared to them. That's not just an expression. The company's main business is preparing and shipping salted salmon. We buy from regular suppliers, the Indians—Cree, Ojibway and Métis—plus French trappers. Then we prepare and salt the salmon, package them in barrels and deliver them to schooners who can only go so far downriver from Port Nelson. The schooners take the fish to coastal ports and across the Atlantic to Europe. Atlantic salmon is very much in demand. Ours come from cold water lakes so they're especially fresh."

"Sounds like a good business," Fargo said.

"Only lately, our shipments are raided regularly. We've been losing a lot of money. I want to find out what's going on," Heather said, her voice hardening.

"Seems like your pa would be on it," Fargo said.

"I heard he went out to do just that and no one's seen him since. That's when I decided to come back," she said.

"Which is first, your pa or the business?" Fargo asked.

Her eyes narrowed at him. "Why'd you ask that?"

"Sixth sense," he said honestly.

Her eyes stayed on him, appraising. "You're good, maybe too good," she said.

"You want to cancel me out?" Fargo questioned.

"Oh, no, I'm going to need everything you have to bring to this," Heather said. "As to your question, yes, I've my own reasons. I own half the company. Mother left it to me when she died. Now, have I cleared that up?"

"I'd say so," Fargo agreed as Heather maneuvered her horse in a sharp right turn. The wide expanse of Lake Winnipeg loomed up ahead.

"We'll take the flatboat at Jackhead," Heather said and led the way past a half-dozen shacks that edged the shore of the big lake. Fargo saw the flatboat tied at the shore, a small paddle wheel at the stern. Heather spoke to the boatman and moved the dapple-grey onto the boat. Fargo followed. He dismounted with her at the port side of the boat by a gunwale raised hardly six inches. It wasn't long before a dozen more customers boarded, some young couples, two older couples with their traveling bags. Most were on foot but there were a few more horses that boarded. The last to board was a man on a bay gelding, a thin-faced figure wearing a jacket and a black Stetson. He took a spot at the stern near the paddle wheel and dismounted.

The boatman finally cast off, turned on a small steam engine that powered the paddle wheel and guided his boat out into the center of the lake. Fargo found Heather leaning against him as the boat moved at a slow crawl, and she continued in her role of guide, pointing out the beauties of the lake. "We're passing through Lynx Bay," she said. "That's Reindeer Island over there. Do you see the ospreys beyond it?" He nodded and she went on. "There's a whole colony who've sort of transplanted themselves from the sea."

"How long since you've been back here?" he asked.

"A few years. I can't really remember. I lost track of time," she said.

Fargo smiled inwardly as he thought of her answers regarding Ernie Binder and the derringer. She had a way of giving glib, reasonable explanations that turned aside questions rather than answering them. "Where were you during those years?" he asked.

"Traveling here and there, wandering about," she said. Fargo smiled inwardly again.

"You visit the States?"

"No. Wanted to but never got there," she said and returned her eyes to the lake that stretched out northward before the boat. Fargo let his gaze sweep over the other passengers. They were all busy gazing across the water, all except the thin-faced man at the stern with the bay gelding. His eyes were fixed on Heather, boring into her. He quickly looked away when he became aware of Fargo's eyes on him. Fargo's brow furrowed as he looked out across the waters of Lake Winnipeg. The boat continued its slow path northward, the thump of the paddle wheel almost hypnotic. When Fargo looked back to the stern again, the thin-faced man's eyes were still peering at Heather and once again he turned away at Fargo's glance.

But his eyes had been piercing, a frown on his brow. Fargo leaned closer to Heather. "Don't be obvious but check the man at the stern with the bay gelding. Do you know him?" he asked. Heather casually glanced around the boat before answering.

"Never saw him before," she murmured.

"He keeps looking hard at you," Fargo said.

She returned a half smile, an edge of smugness in it. "Men looking at me is not exactly an unusual thing," she murmured.

Fargo felt the concession in his own smile. "I'm sure of that," he said.

"That's all it is. Take my word for it," Heather said and linked her arm in his. "We'll be getting off at the last stop, Limestone Point. From there we go across the lakes that are all over this part of Rupert's Land. Sometimes, I'll want you to chase down your own leads. I'll be following others and making contact with some of our posts. We'll compare notes and save time that way."

"Sounds good enough," Fargo said and Heather stayed on his arm as the flatboat moved its slow way forward. It soon halted at a place called Dancing Point, then went on to Wicked Point. A few of the other passengers debarked at one or another of the stops. But the thin-faced man with the bay gelding stayed aboard, Fargo noted. The sun had slid into late afternoon when the boat finally nosed into the narrow finger of land called Limestone Point. Fargo saw the man lead his horse from the boat and followed with the Ovaro and Heather on her dapple-grey. The narrow spit of land was crowded with wagons, mostly sturdy one-horse farm wagons, and a crowd of woodsmen. Travelers with their bags and trappers carrying their packs moved along as well, some leading mules. Fargo's eyes sought out the thin-faced man but he couldn't find him. He searched the narrow strip of land, seeing everyone else that had left the boat. But the thin-faced man was nowhere.

He had disappeared, so completely that it had to have been done swiftly and on purpose. Fargo frowned as uneasiness stabbed at him. He drew alongside Heather and saw shadows begin to lengthen as she led the way to the end of the thin point of land and onto terrain that was soft, with a swampy feel to it underfoot. She turned and headed straight north, and the ground quickly grew firmer. When she brought them into a heavy forest of balsam fir, she turned to him and said, "You pick a place to camp."

Fargo cast another glance at the sky. "We've a good while yet," he said and kept a steady pace through the strong fragrance of the balsams. But as he rode, his eyes scanned the trees behind them and on both sides. Was his uneasiness unwarranted? he asked himself. Perhaps, he admitted, yet it continued to nag at him and he swore inwardly. He had long ago learned to trust the power of his sixth sense and he cast another glance at the gathering dusk. "We going to keep on heading north?" he asked.

"For a while, at least till tomorrow," Heather replied.

"You keep on. I'll catch up to you," he said.

"Where are you going?" She frowned at once.

"Want to check around," Fargo answered.

29

Her frown stayed. "You think we're being followed by the man from the flatboat," she said. He let silence answer for him. "I told you he was just looking," she said dismissively.

"There were a lot of wild-looking characters on the point. They were all looking hard at you. I don't like surprises," Fargo said.

"You worry too much," Heather mocked.

"I'm getting paid for it," he said, and she smiled.

"Don't be long," she said.

"I won't be," he said and rode from her. He retraced their steps but went into the trees to the right of the path by which they had travelled. He slowed to a walk and crisscrossed the ground they had ridden. When the light began to fade, he dismounted and went on foot. Suddenly he halted as the prints appeared at the right of the trail. A lone rider, he saw, and quickly remounted the Ovaro and followed the horse's prints. They seemed to follow his and Heather's trail. But the rider hadn't tracked directly behind them, Fargo noted. That would have made him more vulnerable to being spotted.

Instead, he'd followed them from one side. He knew how to track, Fargo grimaced. But that only meant he could be any of the trappers and hunters that had crowded Limestone Point. His face drawn tight, Fargo followed the prints of the lone rider as the dusk turned deeper, finally relenting to darkness. Dismounting again, he searched on foot under the weak moonlight that fought its way through the balsam forest. Finally he stopped trying to find prints and peered into the night to find the darker shape of a horse and rider. But he saw nothing and realized that the rider had turned away. He suspected that their pursuer gave up after trying to follow prints in the forest darkness. Fargo also turned away, moving to where his and Heather's prints led northward and followed. Finally he heard the sound of Heather's grey just ahead.

He put the pinto into a trot and caught up to her. She heard him approach and was facing him as he came into sight, her hand half behind her saddlebag in front of her. He saw the concern slide from her face as she saw him. "It's about time," she snapped. "I was getting worried."

"Sorry," he apologized.

"Find anyone?"

"No," he said, deciding not to alarm her more than he already had. He glanced around at the spot where she had halted. "This is a good enough place to bed down," he said, and she slid from the dapple-grey at once. She unsaddled the horse and pulled a blanket from her saddlebag. When he finished unsaddling the Ovaro, she had sticks of dried deer meat in hand and gave him one.

"We flavor it with ground up berries," she said as he took one.

"Sort of what we call pemmican," he said. "Where are we going from here?" he asked as they ate.

"We've a post at the edge of Cross Lake. We'll be stopping there," Heather said, finishing her dried deer strip and getting to her feet. "I'm tired. Didn't get much sleep last night, as you know. You must be, too."

"A little," he conceded and watched her arrange her blanket as he set out his bedroll. The moon had risen higher but the balsams still refused to allow much light in. She turned her back to him, pulled off her sweater and Levis, enabling him a glimpse of a strong, well-shaped back, and a firm rear below a narrow waist before she drew a nightgown around herself.

"Good night, Fargo," she said as she folded herself into the blanket. "I'm glad you're along."

"I'm glad you're glad," he said, stretching out and waiting until he heard the steady sound of sleep in her breathing. He rose, then quietly took the Ovaro and his bedroll and drew the horse deeper into a thicket, tethering it there. Moving away, he set his bedroll down a dozen yards from where Heather slept. He no longer wondered if he was being unduly cautious. Someone had followed them for a good part of the way, at least. That was more than enough for him to be wary, and he stretched out on his bedroll, his glance going to Heather where she slept in the more open spot. Anyone coming up on her wouldn't also take him by surprise, which is exactly what would happen if he were still bedded down near her.

That was all he'd need. He'd hear her as she was awakened and be able to do his own surprising. Maybe the night would pass without an intruder. Yet there was never any harm in taking precautions. He lay back and closed his eyes, felt weariness wrap itself around him, and fell into sleep. He had no idea how long he'd been asleep when he woke. But there'd been no noise from Heather, no surprised gasps. He was awakened by something hard and cold pressed into the side of his neck. He blinked, and took a second to identify the touch against his neck. It was the muzzle of a six-gun. A man's voice came next, almost an admiring tone to it.

"Not bad, mister. It would've worked with most,"

the voice said. "Don't do anything dumb. I've an itchy trigger finger." Fargo stayed frozen in place, his lips drawn. Fargo felt the man's hand move to his holster and pull his Colt out. Fargo gave a moment's thought to grabbing for the weapon, but the cold pressure on his neck told him it was a thought to discard. When the man had the Colt out of the holster, he stepped back a pace and Fargo felt the six-gun being drawn away from his neck. He turned to see the thin-faced man under a black Stetson. Fargo cursed inwardly. He had underestimated the man. Not only did he know how to track, he was an experienced hunter, aware of the tricks the hunted used for self-protection. He stared at the man's hollow cheeks, which added a gaunt severity to his face. "Get up," the man ordered and Fargo pushed to his feet.

"Who are you?" he asked.

"I ask the questions," the man said, and Fargo heard Heather stir and push herself up on one elbow.

"Fargo?" she called. "Where are you?"

"He's right here, girlie," the man called and Heather rose to her feet. "Stay right there or he gets shot," the thin-faced man warned. He shot a glance at Fargo. "I figure you're a bodyguard or a boyfriend. Give me any trouble and you'll be a dead one, whichever you are." He gestured to Heather with his head. "Get dressed. It's over, girlie," he growled.

"What's over?" Fargo asked.

"She knows," the man said.

"I don't know what you're talking about," Heather snapped.

"Your plans, honey, whatever they were," the thin man said.

33

"Because you've your own plans for me," Heather said.

"Damn right," the man replied and shifted the gun at Fargo as Heather turned her back to him and started to dress. "Turn around," he ordered Fargo. "I'm putting you in irons. That'll save me the trouble of shooting you."

"While you're enjoying the girl," Fargo said.

"While I do what I came to do," the man rasped, and Fargo cursed silently as he felt the shackles close around his wrists. Leg irons would be next, he knew, and he tightened his leg muscles to prepare. A well-aimed kick could change things in an instant. But once again, the man showed his experience. "On your knees, mister. I don't take chances," he said. Fargo swore helplessly as he was pushed to his knees, his opportunity and leverage gone as he felt the shackles snap around his ankles. The man stepped away and started to move toward Heather, who still had her back to him. "Now for you, honey," he said, holstering his six-gun.

Fargo saw Heather turn to the man, still holding her blanket in one hand, the hazel eyes narrowed, suddenly holding a piercing iciness in them he had never seen before. He didn't see the gun but heard it fire from under the blanket, two quick shots sounding almost as one. Once again, he heard the soft sound of a derringer. The man's body shuddered. "Goddamn," he groaned as he fell to his knees. "Bitch," he managed to add. Heather hadn't been close enough for a derringer's most effective range, and Fargo saw the man struggling to get to his feet. Heather quickly stepped forward, raised the gun to fire again.

"No, wait. Wait," Fargo shouted. But Heather

pulled the trigger, and fired two more shots. The man pitched forward onto his thin face and lay still. "Damn," Fargo swore. "I thought we could get something out of him."

Heather shrugged. "Sorry," she said. She let the blanket fall aside.

"You said somebody found the derringer," Fargo frowned.

"I didn't say I didn't have another," she said and Fargo saw her fingers were clasped around a slightly larger Sharps four-barreled derringer, all steel except for the grips. It was indeed another gun, and she calmly stuffed it into the waistband of her Levi's.

"You're made of surprises," Fargo said.

"You ought to be glad that I am," she returned.

"Guess so," he conceded. "But you didn't even believe we were being followed. He'd have had us both if I'd listened to you. You ought to be glad that I didn't."

"Guess so," she sniffed. "But you used me as bait, dammit."

"Only so he wouldn't catch us both in the same net," Fargo returned.

"It didn't work out the way you planned," she said.

"No, it didn't. I knew he was good by the way he tracked us. He was even smarter than I expected," Fargo said. "Now, you want to see if he has the keys to these irons in his pocket?"

She knelt beside the man's body and started to go through his pockets. She didn't need to go through more than the first trouser pocket when she found the small key on its own chain. She tried it on his wrist irons and they sprung open. He took the keys and freed himself from the ankle irons, pushed to his feet, and went to the man's still figure. "Let's see what else he had on him," Fargo muttered. He started to go through the man's pockets, and drew out a stiff square of paper and held it up to the moonlight. "Stanley Rabb, Special Officer, MACI," Fargo read aloud. "Shit, he was a lawman. An outfit called MACI. What's that mean?"

"Haven't any idea," Heather said.

"Why was he chasing you down?" Fargo questioned.

"Earning his living. He was paid to stop me. What makes you think lawmen can't be bought? It just takes money and connections. I'm not surprised." Fargo stared back and knew he was unable to disagree.

"Let's get away from here," he said and Fargo went into the thick woods and retrieved the Ovaro as a sourness stayed in his mouth. Heather's answer had been entirely reasonable yet again he was bothered. He'd been part of a lawman's death, and though he might have been a corrupt one, he wished he'd had a chance to hear the man out. But Heather had seen her chance to put an end to that, and he couldn't blame her. She had acted in the heat of the moment, and saved his bacon to boot.

Waiting on the grey when he returned, she rode in silence beside him as they cantered into the new day. He found a small brook and halted. "We can finish sleeping here," he said and soon he lay not far from her as the trees kept the brightest rays of the sun out. He woke before noon and glanced over at Heather. Asleep, she looked peacefully innocent. It was hard to see her as being as calm and quick with words and derringers as she had proven to be. She was an intriguing mixture he decided. She woke as he was at the stream filling his canteen, his thoughts still on the man from the night before. He turned as she knelt down beside him.

"He was a lawman and that bothers you," she said.

"Does it show that much?" He frowned.

"No, but the idea of a rotten lawman bothers you. It's part of who you are," she said and her hand caressed his cheek, a soft, tender touch. "None of us can escape who we are," she said softly, a sudden tenderness in her touch and her voice.

"It doesn't bother you?" he asked.

She surprised him with a quick laugh that held a harsh note in it. "Nothing bothers me anymore. Best self-protection there is," she said. She was probably right, he conceded inwardly and rose to his feet. The sun was high when he rode beside her, leaving the balsam forest to cross a long stretch of open land dotted with stands of jack pine. Fields of purple prairie clover were in stark contrast to the harsh, ragged, sternness of the pines. "Only a few hours more to Cross Lake," Heather said at one point as she turned northeast.

"You expect your pa might be there?" Fargo questioned.

"No, Cross Lake's just an outpost. Besides, he wouldn't be anywhere I might be," she said.

"But you're going back to help him," Fargo said.

"I'm going back to help myself, as you suspected. That'll help him too, but he won't welcome it," she said. "We never got along," she added as an icy coldness took over her voice. Again, he was conscious of the mixture of her unexpected tenderness and sudden

37

harshness. They rode until the afternoon sun was starting its slow path toward the horizon, and soon he saw the body of clear blue water come into sight. "Cross Lake," she announced, the lake much larger and longer than he'd expected, stretching like a long, somewhat misshapen finger. He saw a large, unpainted shack and three smaller ones near it. A dozen figures, men and women, were at work at the shore, some repairing canoes, others stretching hides. He noted a half-dozen large salmon laid out in wood trays filled with water, the strong odor of salt rising to his nostrils.

He was staring at the size and magnificence of the salmon as Heather's voice cut in, "Beautiful, aren't they? *Ouananiche*," she said. He frowned back. "The Indian word for the Atlantic salmon. They're called that all over Canada."

Fargo's eyes went to the figures at the shore. "They Indian?" he queried.

"They're Métis," she said and he frowned back. "To be a Métis you have to be half Indian and half European descent. We trade with Cree, Ojibway and Assiniboine. We also buy from the French hunters and trappers who call themselves the *coureurs de bois*, the wood runners, but our workers are all Métis."

"It seems they're friendlier than the American tribes," Fargo said.

"Not always. The Métis have been part of two major uprisings led by a firebrand, Louis Riel, but my Father was able to work out a good relationship with them. They do the real preparing and shipping at our posts along the river."

"Only one river?"

"Mostly the Nelson, which winds all the way down

from Port Nelson on Hudson Bay where the schooners wait for our deliveries," Heather said. "But we'll be visiting there soon enough. Now let's see what we have here."

She started for the largest of the shacks, then halted and dismounted there. Fargo followed as she approached the closed door. His hand reached for her elbow. "I don't think it's a good idea to walk in the front door, not with what's already happened," he said.

She halted. "Maybe not," she agreed. "There's a side door. We'll try that instead." He nodded and his hand was on the butt of his Colt as Heather reached for the knob of the smaller side door.

3

Heather's hand turned the doorknob, and the door swung open. Fargo entered with her, quickly took in a large room with file cabinets, boxes, an old, battered desk and two wooden chairs. Fishing poles, axes, shovels, rakes, and snowshoes were stacked in one corner and piles of netting dotting the floor. A man with short, brown hair and very pale skin turned as Heather stepped forward, surprise flooding his face. His thin figure stiffened. "By God," he murmured.

"Hello, Sam," Heather said. "Glad to see me?"

"Sure, sure, of course," the man said, plainly still flustered. "We always got on. You know that," he said and Fargo heard the definite Scottish brogue in his voice.

"This is Sam Simpson, Fargo," Heather introduced. "Sam has been our agent here at the Cross Lake post for many years." Sam Simpson nodded, and Fargo saw him still staring at Heather, shock in his face. "Been hearing things," Heather said. "What do you know about the robberies, Sam?"

Simpson pulled himself together. "Only that they keep happening. Not around here, though. Along the Nelson," he said.

Heather turned to Fargo. "That's where you'll be scouting," she said.

"What about you?" Fargo frowned.

"I'll be with you when I can but there are some things I want to check out on my own. It'll be better that way," she said.

"We'll talk more about this," Fargo muttered and Heather turned to Sam Simpson.

"I'll want a good night's rest. Is the extra shack in order?" she queried.

"Yes, it's still kept for visitors," Sam Simpson said, his very pale skin even paler, Fargo thought.

"Is Rory Dermott still in charge of the north Sipi-wesk post?" Heather asked, and Simpson nodded. "He'll know more about these robberies. I'll be paying him a visit," she said. Fargo saw something close to alarm flood Sam Simpson's face as he gazed at Heather.

"You think you need to do that?" he asked. "Rory can handle things."

"I wouldn't go otherwise," Heather said, her tone growing sharp. "My bag's outside. I'll be going to the shack now," Heather said curtly.

Simpson turned to the side door when the front door of the main shack opened and another girl stepped in. Perhaps blew in was more accurate, Fargo decided, as she came in with a flourish, filling the room with her presence. Shoulder-length, shiny, thick black hair framed a face comprised of strong cheekbones, a thin, straight nose, a wide mouth, and a sensual face wrapped in coppery olive skin. Only her eyes startled him. Though her dark complexion seemed to warrant that they be flashing black orbs, they were a sparkling light blue.

A white, low-necked blouse rested on deep breasts and a black wool skirt covered womanly hips. Everything about her simmered like a banked fire. Hands on hips, her light-blue eyes swept the room, holding an instant longer on Fargo. "I only expected Sam," she said and Fargo frowned at an accent he couldn't pinpoint. "*Quelle surprise,*" she added in French.

"Yes, a surprise," Sam Simpson said. "This is Heather Grandy. You know the family name, of course."

"*Oui,*" the young woman said, the accent not quite like any French accent he had heard; Fargo frowned. It was flatter, harsher.

"This is Heather's friend, Skye Fargo," Simpson said. "This is my assistant, Monique."

Fargo caught Heather's sharp, probing stare at the young woman. "You are Métis," Heather said.

"*Oui,*" Monique said and Fargo wondered if the pride in the single word was real or defensive.

Sam Simpson's voice cut into his thoughts. "Monique knows more about this land than most guides, hunters, trappers, Indians, or wood runners. That's why I made her my assistant," he said.

"Then maybe she can help Fargo. He's here to get a hold on the attacks on our shipments," Heather said.

Monique's glance at Fargo held appraisal and approval in her sky-blue eyes. "I can try," she purred.

"I want to turn in," Heather said to Simpson as the last of the day began to fade. "You've a place for Fargo?"

"The last shack. There's a cot in it and an overhang behind for his horse," the man said.

"That'll do fine," Fargo said as Simpson followed Heather outside. Fargo turned to see Monique studying him.

"You know her well? You are an old friend?" she asked.

"Wouldn't say that. She hired me. I'm good at finding things. Some people call me the Trailsman," Fargo said.

"You are *un Americain*," Monique said, and Fargo nodded.

"What kind of Métis are you?" he asked.

"Cree and French," she said. "This Heather, she is of the Grandy family."

"That's right. You've never heard of her?"

"Never. I met *Pere* Grandy twice. The Grandys have big business. I am a little nobody," Monique said as Sam Simpson returned and lit a lamp before the room became engulfed in darkness.

"You're in the last shack, Fargo," Simpson said gruffly.

"See you tomorrow, big *Americain*," Monique said, a smile edging her lovely lips. He felt her eyes on him as he left the big shack. Outside, night had descended and he found the last of the shacks. He unsaddled the Ovaro and tied the horse under the overhang in the back. A narrow cot was the only piece of furniture inside, and he ate a stick of dried beef from his saddlebag in the blackness of the little room, then undressed and stretched. Sleep came quickly and he didn't wake until a lone window let in a shaft of morning sunlight. He washed in the waters of Cross Lake, then dressed and saddled the pinto before walking to the main shack.

He heard Monique's voice through the partly ajar

door, petulant irritation in her tone. "I told you, I don't know where he went. He was gone when I got here."

Heather's voice answered with a sharp sneer. "You're his helper around here and he said nothing to you about leaving? I've trouble believing that," she said.

"Believe whatever you want," Monique snapped as Fargo pulled the door open and entered. Heather turned to him.

"Sam Simpson's taken off," she said. "I don't like this."

"Why would he do that?" Fargo asked Monique.

"I don't know. It worries me, too," she said.

"I'll find out," Heather said with ice in her voice.

"I have things to do," Monique said and walked from the shack.

"I don't believe she doesn't know anything about this," Heather said to Fargo. "I'm going to Rory Dermott at north Sipiwesk."

"You want me to go along?" Fargo queried.

"No. I want you to stay here and find out what you can from Monique. I want to see Rory alone. I don't want him knowing about you, not yet. You're my secret weapon," she said.

"You suspect this Rory Dermott's involved in the robberies?" Fargo asked.

"I don't know," she said. "I'm not ruling out anybody." Fargo walked outside with her to where the dapple-grey waited. "Find out more about Monique. Maybe she and Sam Simpson are involved. She's too nervous about his running out. Let her take you around, keep poking at her." She climbed onto the horse and rode off at a gallop. When Fargo returned to the shack, he found Monique inside, her blue eyes flashing.

"I don't like her," she snapped. "Not just because she doesn't believe me."

Fargo studied her for a moment, deciding she wasn't pretending. "Not everybody likes everybody else," he said in an effort to be both honest and disarming. "It's your privilege."

"There's something about her . . ." Monique said and made a dour face.

"But you can't blame her for being suspicious. Most people would expect Sam Simpson to tell you he was taking off," Fargo said, keeping his voice reasonable.

Monique frowned back. "I know. That is why I am so worried. He has a bad heart. That is why he is so pale. He should not go running off by himself. He is not well enough."

"Why do you think he did?" Fargo asked.

"I do not know," Monique said, plainly upset. "Sam has been so good to me. I am very worried over this."

"Maybe he'll be back soon," Fargo said.

"No, I feel it inside. Something is wrong. That is why he went without telling me," she insisted.

"Stop worrying. Get your mind on something else," Fargo said. "Heather wants you to show me around, show me the way to the salmon shipment routes."

"I can't. I have to stay here and mind the office. It is what Sam would want. Trappers bring in their lists for payment. I have to go over each one," she said and he saw the nervousness move across her face, her fingers clenching. He moved a step back to the desk where a sheaf of papers rested under a stone paper-weight. He took in the long list of items on the top sheet, each one checked off.

"These the lists?" he asked.

"Yes. You see they are long. They will take work," she said.

"But these are all finished, all checked off," he said.

She pressed one hand over the top list, and he saw her lips tighten. "These are last week's. I have to wait for the new ones," she said quickly. She was plainly lying, he grunted inwardly, tossing off quick, convenient answers. "You can look for the routes yourself. You said they call you the Trailsman. You can find your way," she went on.

Fargo smiled back. "It'd help if you came along," he said calmly.

"I'll show you which direction to go. You don't need me," she said and couldn't help looking pleased with herself.

"Guess that'll have to do," Fargo said blandly and she followed him outside to the Ovaro, where he pulled himself into the saddle.

"Just ride north," Monique said. "You'll reach Lake Sipiwesk. Many trappers, hunters and wood runners stop there with their catch."

He smiled at her. "I'd still like it if you came along."

A tiny light rose in her blue eyes. "I would like that, too. But another time," she said.

"See you when I get back," he said and put the pinto into a trot. His thoughts held on Monique as he rode. She had shown both honesty and deceit and tried to mask both behind her simmering beauty. But not well enough. Her feelings about Heather had been real, but she had lied about having to stay in the shack, and she'd jumped at the chance to send him on his way. That danger signal was more than enough for him, Fargo knew. She was very troubled and very nervous, and that always made for problems.

He slowed, turned to glance back, and swore. There were no trees or tall brush anywhere near the shacks. The land along the shore of the lake was open and flat. There was no way he could sneak back to the shack without being seen. "Damn," he muttered and rode on until he came to a cluster of scraggly white pine. Riding into the trees, he halted and swung from the saddle. Peering back the way he had come, he could see the figures on the shore of the lake, with the main shack behind them. Lowering himself to the ground, Fargo settled down, certain he only had to watch and wait. But the hours dragged on with no activity except for the Métis on the shore repairing their canoes. Fargo watched the distant figures and wondered if Sam Simpson might just return.

The sun had sunk into the late afternoon sky when he saw Monique come from the shack, hurry to a horse tethered at one side and ride away. She headed northeast, following the edge of Cross Lake. Fargo climbed onto the Ovaro and rode from the trees, letting Monique ride out of sight. He wanted to be certain that she wouldn't glance back and spot him. When he reached the shack, he picked up her hoofprints and followed their trail in the soft soil near the lake. The prints stayed clear when she turned from the lake and crossed land dotted with low, scraggly bushes, passing several small clusters

47

of white pine and juniper. Day began to fade, quickly becoming the soft grey of twilight. He increased the pace of the Ovaro and closed the distance behind Monique. When night fell, he was close enough to her to dismount and follow her on foot.

The moon rose to help him, and he found the hoofprints of her horse, seeing where she had wandered to the east, then to the west. He moved slowly, pausing often to let his fingers feel the prints in the ground and make sure he had the right ones. Temperature and texture told him when he made a mistake, and it was perhaps another hour when he suddenly froze in place. The sound of a horse blowing air through its nose came to him, not far ahead. He listened and the horse snorted again. The horse was standing still, relaxed, the sound very different from that of a horse blowing on the move. Fargo moved forward again, on soft, careful steps. Finally he saw the figure on the ground, wrapped in a blanket.

She was hard asleep when he reached her, and he knelt down on one knee and pressed one hand over her mouth. She came awake instantly, eyes wide with surprise. "It's just me," he said and drew his hand away. She sat up at once, and he glimpsed the swell of her breasts as her blouse hung open. She pulled it closed with one hand as her eyes peered at him with a grudging respect.

"You are very good, Trailsman," she said.

"You weren't hard to follow," Fargo said. "I think you'd better start talking."

"I came looking for Sam," she said.

"You follow his trail?" Fargo questioned.

"No, I am not that good. But I knew this is the way he would have gone."

"Gone where?" Fargo pushed at her.

"Maybe the north Sipiwesk post. Maybe the main office at Split Lake."

"You've still no idea why he left?" Fargo asked suspiciously.

"No. I came because I'm afraid for him. That's the truth, Fargo. I just want to find him before he does too much and his heart gives out," Monique said and reached up, her hands pressed against his chest. Her blouse fell open enough for him to see the edges of two lovely, full, curving mounds. "Help me. You are very good. You could find his trail. Please, Fargo," she begged.

"Finding his trail by the moonlight would be hard," he told her.

"You found me," she said.

"That was different. I was on your tail," he said.

"Try, please try," she pleaded, hands tightening against his chest. It was no act, he felt certain, the anxiety in her face was too real. "Maybe he is not far ahead, stopped for the night, too."

"I'll give it a try," he said and her arms flew around his neck, her softness pressing into him for a moment.

"Thank you, thank you," she said. She stepped back and began to close the buttons on her blouse. "He would have gone across here, to the northeast. It is the shortest way," she said as she finished tucking clothes in. Fargo stayed on foot as Monique climbed onto the dapple-grey.

"Stay behind me," he said. The Ovaro would follow along, he knew, as he stepped out briskly. The flat land continued to be heavily dotted with small, scrubby shrubs, an occasional stand of white pine, and small ponds that shimmered under the moon. He scanned every shrub he passed, but over an hour had gone by when he finally spotted what he searched for. The edges of two shrubs were crushed and broken by a horse's hoofs. He moved on, found the hoofprints and more crushed shrubs. They turned right toward a cluster of pines and a large pond. He spotted a horse standing to one side at the edge of the pond and broke into a run as Monique hurried after him.

"It is Sam's horse," she called as he reached the pond. She swung from the grey, but Fargo's eyes were already sweeping the pond, honing in on an object in the water only a few feet from the horse. He waded into the pond, heard Monique's half scream as he pulled Sam Simpson's body from the water. *"Mon dieu, mon dieu!"* she cried out. "Is . . . is he? . . ."

"Yes," Fargo said quietly and heard Monique's stifled sob.

"Poor, poor Sam," she said. "It is what I was afraid might happen. He was riding too hard and his heart gave out as he passed here. He fell from his horse into the pond." She turned away, hands pressed to her lips.

Fargo peered at Sam Simpson. There were no bruises on his face or head. He hadn't fallen and struck a rock. Monique's assessment seemed probably accurate. The man appeared dead, yet Fargo remembered times past when men seemed dead but were in fact still clinging to life. He bent low over Sam Simpson, reached a hand under the man's shirt to his chest as he lowered one ear to listen for a heartbeat, trying to feel for one as well. A furrow came to dig into his brow as his fingers touched something hard and a stickiness clung to his palm. He drew his hand back, and stared at the half-congealed blood on the palm of his hand. Bending low again, he pulled Sam Simpson's shirt open and stared at the end of a black knife handle that protruded from Sam Simpson's shirt. The knife blade had been plunged deep into Simpson's chest. Fargo looked up. Monique's back was still to him, hands still pressed to her lips.

"It was no heart attack," he said softly as she turned, her eyes widening as she stared down at Sam Simpson's body.

"Oh, my God, my God," Monique murmured, shock wreathing her face.

"He was killed and tossed into the pond," Fargo said. "Got any idea who or why?"

"No, no. Sam had no enemies. He was a good man," Monique replied. "Highwaymen. Bandits. We have enough of them around."

Fargo pushed to his feet and his eyes swept the ground in the last of the moonlight before he turned back to the young woman. "There are other tracks here, a single horse," Fargo said. "One killer."

"It only takes one," Monique said bitterly.

Fargo bent down again, this time going through Sam Simpson's pockets. "Nothing. No money. Not even small change," Fargo said when he finished.

"Robbery. Sam always carried some money with him. He wouldn't ride off without money on him," Monique said.

Fargo grimaced as he stared at Sam Simpson. "Whoever did it wanted no noise. He got close enough to use the knife," Fargo said, reaching down and closing one hand around the bloodied hilt. He pulled the knife from Sam Simpson's chest. Fargo plunged it into the pond, watched the water wash the partly-congealed blood from the blade. Finally, he pulled the knife from the water, held it up to the moonlight and frowned at the inscription on the smooth, black hilt of the blade. "Property of MACI," he read aloud. "You know what MACI stands for?" he asked Monique.

"No," she said. "I do not know."

He went to the Ovaro, pulled a kerchief from his saddlebag and wrapped the knife inside it. "I'll hang on to it. Maybe we can find out what they mean. Might be a lead to the killer," he said.

Monique looked down at the still, silent figure. "He had no family, nobody but himself, but we can't leave him here like this."

"Any place to bury him back at the post?" Fargo asked.

"No," she said.

"There's a short-handled spade in my saddlebag. Fetch it," Fargo said as he bent down and lifted the body, carrying it to the edge of a thicket of shrubs. Monique returned with the spade and helped as he dug a shallow grave, laid Sam Simpson in it and used a rock as a headstone. When he was finished, Monique linked her arm in his as they returned to the horses.

"Thank you, Fargo," she murmured. "He was my friend, a good man." Fargo saw the fatigue in her face as she climbed onto her horse and he swung onto the Ovaro.

"You need rest. It's a long ride back. We've a few

hours till day," he said and put the pinto into motion, keeping to a trot until he came to a small but thick stand of juniper. He slowed and nosed the horse into the fragrance of the blue-grey cones as Monique followed. Halting at a little half circle deep inside the trees, he dismounted and unsaddled the Ovaro. "This is a good spot to get some sleep," he said. Monique dismounted and started to tend to her horse. Fargo set out his sleeping bag, pulled off everything but his trousers and stretched out on the bag. Monique had the blanket she was in when he first happened upon her, but she didn't take it from her saddlebag as she came toward him.

"I am very tired but I do not want to sleep alone tonight. You will understand that, I know," she said.

"Why do you know that?" he asked.

"Because you are not like most men. I knew that when I first met you. What you have done tonight proves that," Monique said.

"I understand, but it'll put a strain on my self-discipline," Fargo said as he slid to one side of the bedroll. First Monique pulled off her shirt, the skirt came next leaving only a half-slip. Just enough moonlight filtered through the trees to let him see full, heavy-cupped breasts that swayed together. As she lay down beside him he felt the soft warmth of her. She draped one arm over his chest.

"Thank you, Fargo, for everything," she said softly. "Good night." She closed her eyes and fell asleep in minutes. Her simmering sensuality had vanished. He knew that its disappearance was the only thing that made the moment possible as he took in the soft swell of her breasts. That and his own tiredness pulled him into a deep sleep. His last conscious thoughts were those of amazement over the entirely unexpected twists and turns of human behavior, his own included.

The hours passed in silence and sound sleep, and he woke after the warm sun had found its way through the thickness of the juniper. But it was not the sun that woke him, he realized. It was the soft, caressing touch that moved ever so lightly across his muscled abdomen, down further to his groin. He pulled his eyes open and looked at the figure beside him. No half-slip on any longer, he saw. Thick, black hair fell loosely across his belly as soft lips caressed and provided moist messengers of pleasure. He heard his own moan of satisfaction. Monique raised her head at the sound from him, her eyes meeting his and he saw that all of her shimmering sensuality had returned. He also saw the glow of coppery-olive skin on heavy-cupped breasts, each pinkish brown nipple erect and beckoning. Full-fleshed thighs moved against each other and turned a luxuriously black, thick triangle toward him.

He saw the tiny smile edge Monique's lips as she pulled herself upwards, bringing one soft-firm nipple to his mouth. He opened his lips, drew in the full softness that pressed against him, letting his tongue circle the areola and tracing a path around the edges. Then lightly he touched the very tip with the point of his tongue. Monique gave a half cry and he felt her belly come against his groin, pushing into him. His hand moved down, nestled into the luxurious, filamentous black plumage that covered her venus mound. She was making small, urging sounds and her thighs opened, pressing themselves around him. *"Oui, oui,* ah, ah, yes, yes, yes," she murmured and he could feel the moisture on her thighs, the wine of wanting spilling out of its curving, soft vessel. He let his own pulsating fullness come against her thighs, slid himself forward, and found a portal wide and wanting. Monique cried out in little gasps of delight, as her hands moved up and down his body. She raised her thighs further to take in all of him. "*Oui, oui,* oh, yes, more, more," she moaned.

Moving with him, her body tight against his, she matched his every thrust, twist and motion, making herself a part of him. She cried out at every sensation, her moans growing in strength and pitch. He felt her body tighten with each cry until she began to shudder, letting out a half-whispered scream that seemed to have no end. Her movements grew stronger, her body striking his groin with increasing force until suddenly he heard her voice rise, break, then take on a new fervency. Her hands dug into his shoulders and her thick, jet-black hair fell wildly from side to side as she twisted and half turned. "Oh, *mon dieu,* oh, God. Now, now!" she cried out and he felt her stiffening against him, letting his own desires explode with her. Monique screamed, an ecstacy cry of rapture that circled and then faded away.

She stayed tight against him until her body stopped its stiff clinging, finally falling back as a deep moan escaped her. "Good, yes, yes, good," she whispered and her arms came up to pull his face down to her coppery-olive breasts. He stayed there, enjoying the warmth of her, until finally he moved back, lying down beside her. She turned and draped one arm across his chest. "I do not want you to think it was

55

just for what you did last night," she said. "I knew I would like this to happen from the first time I saw you."

"You always make such quick decisions?" He smiled.

"With you, it was not hard. You are so different from the men who stop at the station," she said.

"Glad you weren't disappointed," Fargo remarked.

"No, no," Monique said, and her hand caressed his chiseled jaw. "And I will help you in every way I can."

"We'd best start back," Fargo said, and he rose, letting her use his canteen to freshen up. Soon she rode beside him as he left the juniper and headed across the open land. He let Monique stay wrapped in her own silence and only when they neared Cross Lake did she find words.

"It will not be the same without Sam there. I do not think I will stay on," she said.

"You've another job?" he queried.

"No, but I'll find one," she said.

"Wait and see what Heather says when she comes back," Fargo advised. Monique didn't answer, he noted. But when they neared the post, Fargo's eyes widened. The front door of the main shack hung open and a tall figure stepped out, wearing a tan vest over a white shirt, the sun catching her deep auburn hair. Fargo halted, Monique beside him as he swung from the Ovaro. "Didn't expect you'd be back so soon," Fargo said to Heather.

"Rory Dermott wasn't at the post. I just turned around and came back here," Heather said. "There was no one here. Where were you?" she asked, turning to Monique.

"I went to see if I could find Sam," Monique said.

"And left the post alone? That's inexcusable," Heather said icily and Monique stiffened. "You find him?" Heather snapped.

"Sam is dead," Monique said and Heather raised one eyebrow. "We found his body in a pond," Monique said.

"We?" Heather said and threw a glance at Fargo.

"I met up with Monique. She asked me to help her look for Sam," Fargo said.

Heather brought her eyes to Monique. "What happened? Accident? His horse throw him?" she questioned.

"No. He was killed. Robbed. Damn highwaymen," Monique said.

"That's what the old fool gets for running off by himself," Heather said callously, and Fargo saw the anger tighten Monique's face. "You'll take over for him here, for now," Heather said.

"I thought you wanted me to help Fargo," Monique said.

"Not now. You'll stay here," Heather said, then spun and strode from the shack as Fargo followed her out to the dapple-grey.

"What are you figuring to do next?" he asked.

"I'm going to talk to some of the Métis who work the south Sipiwesk. Maybe they saw something that might help. They might even have seen my father. I'll decide on our next move then," she said.

"You want company?" Fargo questioned.

"No, they'll talk more if I'm alone," she said and pulled herself into the saddle, riding away without another word, plainly annoyed and displeased. Fargo started back to the shack with the feeling that some of her displeasure included his helping Monique look for Sam Simpson. He entered the shack and found Monique cleaning out a file cabinet, her face tight.

"I won't stay," she threw at Fargo the minute he entered. "I won't work for her."

"I thought you said that you didn't have another job?" he asked.

"I'll find one," Monique shot back.

"Stay for a while. Heather has bigger concerns driving her. She'll be moving on. Wait till this settles down. Someone else may put you in charge here," Fargo said.

"What about you? You will keep working for her," Monique asked.

"I'm still hired. I'll try to help her get the answers she wants. But that doesn't mean you should do anything foolish."

Monique gazed out the window where the day was starting to end. "I'll think about it," she said. "Are you staying at the shack again tonight?"

"Yes," he said.

"You may have company," she murmured.

"That's be nice," he said and Monique's face softened. He left her, went outside and climbed onto the pinto. He rode slowly across the open land, scanning the few travelers he passed. Most were old men driving old carts, a few were trappers with their burros. None fitted the picture of a highwayman, and as the shadows lengthened he turned back toward the shack, arriving as night fell. He found a candle to light and ate a stick of beef jerky. He had stretched out on the cot, the night enfolding the shack in its black blanket, when a knock sounded at the door. "Come in. It's open," he called and swung from the cot as Heather entered. Her light-tan vest rested on her high, full breasts. "Find anything?" he asked her.

"No, but I made plans," she answered. "We'll ride come morning."

"Good," Fargo nodded just as the door opened again and Monique strode in. She halted, stared at Heather in surprise. Fargo saw Heather's eyes narrow at her.

"I'm sorry. I didn't expect anyone," Monique said to Fargo.

"Obviously," Heather snapped. "What are you doing here?"

"Just came to visit," Monique said.

"As you can see, he already has company," Heather said, cold dismissal in her voice. Monique spun on her heel and strode from the shack, slamming the door behind her. Fargo felt Heather's eyes on him.

"Sorry to interrupt your plans," she said icily.

"Didn't have any plans," Fargo said mildly.

"She did," Heather snapped.

"You always jump to conclusions," Fargo tried.

"No jumping. Knowing. A woman knows another woman," Heather said. "And I'm sure you're not a man to turn down an opportunity."

"It's happened," Fargo said.

Her smile was wreathed in skepticism. "Then it'll happen again now. You're working for me. I don't want you laying the help," she said.

"Wouldn't think of it," he said blandly.

"Hell, you wouldn't," she said, and her laugh was edged with hardness. She stepped to him, her lips on his for a brief moment before she stepped back. "Stay in line. You won't regret it," she said. She turned and hurried from the shack without looking back.

Fargo let a wry smile touch his lips as he undressed and returned to the cot. Heather Grandy continued to be a combination of contradictions, callous and cold, quick with glib answers, yet warm, concerned over her father and the business. Contradictory and intriguing.

Fargo rose early, dressed and took the time to give the Ovaro a rubdown, using mostly the dandy brush and hoof pick from his saddlebag. Monique appeared, opening the door of the main shack, and walked to where Fargo was just finished with his horse. "Sorry about last night," she said. Fargo saw more smugness than apology in her face. "She give you trouble?" Monique asked.

"No. Why would she?" Fargo said.

"She is possessive," Monique said.

He gave a wry snort. "Never saw one of you that wasn't."

Monique returned a sniff of rejection. "It's different with her," she said.

"How?" Fargo questioned.

"I don't know," Monique frowned. "But it is."

"You just don't like her," Fargo said.

"No, I am right," Monique snapped and strode back to the shack. Fargo started to put his gear into the saddlebag when Heather came by. She waved at him as she hurried into the main shack and he began to saddle the pinto. He was adjusting the cinch belt when Heather came from the shack and paused beside him.

"I need ten minutes to saddle the grey and tend to a few things, then we'll ride," she said and hurried on. He strolled to the shack and found Monique inside, stuffing a shirt into a sack. She looked up as he entered, her face clouded.

"*Au 'voir*, Fargo," she said. "I have been fired."

"What?" Fargo frowned in surprise.

"*Oui.* She gave me ten minutes to get my things out," Monique said.

"I'll talk to her," Fargo said.

"No, it is just as well. I told you, I do not want to work for her. She comes here, cares nothing about Sam, and just takes over," Monique said with bitterness curling in her voice.

"It's her right. It's her company. Her father she wants to help," Fargo said soothingly. Monique came to him, her arms encircling his neck, her softness pressing against him.

"I am afraid for you, Fargo. Do not work for her. Stay here with me," she said.

"I can't. I made a commitment," he said, and Monique frowned back. "That's like a promise," he said, and she nodded but pressed herself tighter to him.

"Promises can be broken," she murmured.

"Not by me, not without a special reason," Fargo said.

"I am still afraid. There's something about her. I want you to come back to me. I'd like us to be together again," she cooed.

"I'd like that, too. I'll come back. Promise," he said. She took in his words, but there was only dark brooding in her handsome, coppery-olive face. Her lips pressed against his in a warm, intense kiss.

"Go. Be careful," she said almost angrily, and he turned and strode from the shack. Outside, he climbed onto the Ovaro and waited as Heather appeared. She went to the shack and he saw her lock the door, swing onto the grey and come alongside him. He rode with her as she headed north.

"Did she have a tender good-bye for you?" Heather asked disdainfully.

"She said good-bye," Fargo answered. "She doesn't care much for you. She thinks you were cold and callous about Sam Simpson."

"And I don't trust her. She was close to Sam Simpson and I didn't trust him, either. I arrive and he runs off on his own. Why? Maybe he was involved in the robberies," Heather said. "Maybe he ran off to warn somebody." Fargo realized he had no answer—again her conjectures were entirely reasonable. "You saw how surprised he was to see me," she added.

"Being surprised is a normal enough reaction," Fargo said.

"He was more than surprised. He was upset," Heather said and again he had to admit she was right. "I want to find my father, first. The robberies are second to me."

"Maybe they're connected," Fargo said. "Whoever's doing the attacks could have him, sort of as insurance."

She thought for a moment. "I suppose so. I'll think about that," Heather said as she led the way through a long stand of northern white cedar, and Fargo saw the sun slide into the afternoon as they rode. "We're going to the Nelson River. I asked around and most of the attacks have been along the river. It's still narrow there. It doesn't widen until it reaches Sundance."

Fargo watched the sun move on and the shadows lengthen.

"When do we reach this place?" he asked.

"In the morning," she said as they slowed to let a herd of elk cross in front of them. They were near another stand of white cedar, and he felt a chill come in with the gathering darkness. He turned into the cedars as Heather followed and pulled into a small open circle inside the trees.

"I think a fire will be in order tonight," Fargo said.

"When you head north, the nights turn cool," Heather said and swung from the grey. Fargo found plenty of loose wood and had a small fire blazing in minutes. He set out his bedroll as night fell. The fire warmed the little circle at once and Heather stretched as the firelight touched her deep auburn hair.

"You might not need your blanket," Fargo said.

"I wasn't intending to use it anyway," she said. "Your bedroll will hold two."

"So it will," he said. She turned, lit by the fire, and began to shed clothes in slow, graceful movements until she was standing beautifully naked in front of him. Soft curves all over, a tall figure, well-filled yet lithesome. Her high breasts curved to pear-shaped cups, her skin almost ivory, setting off deep pink nipples and areolas. A thin waist funneled down to beautifully curved legs and a wide, bushy triangle that was also touched with auburn. Ivory skin glowing in the firelight, she came toward him, a slight smile edging her lips. "You didn't seem like the impulsive type," he commented.

"I'm not being impulsive. I'm just doing what I want to do," she said. She came to him and pressed herself against him as she helped him shed his clothes, staying against him as he lay back on the bedroll. She was warm; her smooth ivory skin shuddered at his touch. He found one high breast, drew it into his mouth and let his lips play with the deep-pink nipple. "Oh, oh, ooooh," Heather groaned, her voice low. He circled the soft top with his tongue, caressed gently, pulled and sucked. Heather began to moan, deep, long moans and her body surged forward, a slow, sinuous movement. As his lips and hands explored and roamed across her body, her moans stayed low, almost purring growls, and she turned and twisted her hips, torso, and belly. "Ah, aaaaaaah," Heather groaned as his hand probed downward, arriving at the auburn-tinted triangle.

He pressed down on the soft venus mound and ran fingers through soft-wire tendrils as Heather's deep, low moans grew in intensity. He explored further, his fingertips reaching the softness of skin at the edge of her waiting portal. Heather clutched at him and let loose a throaty growl. Her hips gyrated as her ivory-skinned thighs fell open. "Yes, yes," she cried, her voice a dusky whisper. He half turned, brought his own throbbing to her, rested for a moment at the edge of the warm, moist gift, and Heather moaned again, a surprisingly soft sound. He slid forward, slowly, and her cries deepened. Her body moved, rose with him, welcoming, giving, joining.

He started gently, then moved with a deeper intensity as Heather's deep howls rose with him. Her entire body rocked with his, slow, surging movements, intense yet relaxed, every part of her clinging to him, rubbing against him. As she surged, she brought her high, full breasts to his face, rubbing them up and down across his lips, then kissed him full on the lips as the wave of her body crashed into him again. The deep, carnal snarls matched every surge of her body, sound and flesh harmonizing, one echoing the other, her low growls both exciting and encompassing. Her surgings growing stronger every moment, he felt his own passion rise, demanding its own fulfillment. She was humming along like a locomotive's engine, with a sound that only rose in intensity as her body twisted, turned, rose and fell again. Suddenly he felt her thighs tighten around him.

Her slow, serpentine surging didn't change character even though her entire body tightened around him. The growl tore from somewhere deep inside her, a guttural cry, and he felt himself exploding with her as her auburn-tinted pubic mound pushed hard into his groin. "Ah, ah, aaaaah, yes, yes. . . . ah, yes!" Heather wailed and she quivered hard against him, every part of her shaking, clinging, her ivory skin suddenly moist, helping her adhere to him. She groaned and clung, all of her pushing, holding, quivering in a kind of growling ecstacy, moans straining with pleasure until he heard her final sigh coming from deep inside her that made her entire body shudder and suddenly lie silent. Slowly, she drew from him and lay back, deep breaths escaping from her lips. "Good, oh, God, so good," she murmured, her arms staying around him, keeping him pressed against her high, full breasts.

When her arms finally slid from around him, she lay on her back for a moment, then pushed up onto one elbow, and he saw the satisfied little smile that edged her lips, a quiet victory curling inside it. "Now you'll know," she murmured.

"Know what?" He frowned.

"That you won't need to bother with any other Moniques you might meet," she said.

"You expect I'll meet others?" he queried.

"Girls like Monique are all over the provinces. You'll have no need to be tempted, now," Heather said.

"Definitely not," Fargo agreed and pressed into her ivory-skinned softness. She slid upwards, bringing her breasts to his lips.

"Sleep tight," she said and closed her eyes, and in moments he heard the steady sound of her breathing as she fell asleep, her breasts still to his lips. He pulled sleep around himself as well, feeling her shift during the night to lie beside him. She was still asleep when he woke with the morning, slid from the bedroll and dressed. The new sun sent little sparks of auburn from her hair as it bathed her ivory skin in a soft glow. Waking her, he saddled the horses as she dressed, met the warmth of her lips when she finished and saw the satisfied little light still dancing in her eyes. She climbed into the saddle and led the way north, and he found a sizeable growth of raspberry and pin cherry that furnished breakfast. It turned out to be almost a full day's ride before they reached their destination. Heather gestured to a long, narrow river. "The Nelson. See how narrow it is here? We're just north of Lake Sipiwesk," she said.

He nodded as he took in a half-dozen long, heavy wood tables at the river's edge. Rows of women, and a few men, were working with barrels smelling of brine beside each table. They were piled high with Atlantic salmon and Fargo followed Heather as she dismounted and walked alongside the tables. "These are part of our workers. They're all Métis," Heather said.

"They're gutting the fish, as you can see. They split the bodies then remove the backbones and adjoining bony parts. We used to cut off the heads but now we leave them on, they keep better that way. Besides, some of the schooner captains who service the Asian trade want the heads left on. Once the salmon are gutted, they're packed in barrels with brine for shipment to the major ports along the Atlantic coast. Schooners crossing the Atlantic repack the fish in ice."

Fargo's glance cut to the huddle of flat-bottomed boats and large canoes that were tied together. "You use those dugouts and canoes to take the barrels to the schooners?" he queried.

"That's right," she said and Fargo watched some of the women put heavy lids atop each packed barrel.

"And once you deliver the barrels, the captains of the schooners pay you," Fargo said.

"The inspectors come first," she said. "There are government inspectors aboard every ship. They check the barrels to see that they hold what we claim they are."

"What are they looking for?"

"Expensive furs and pelts in barrels marked salmon, sometimes even guns."

"And after the barrels are cleared?" Fargo questioned.

"We're paid the going rate for each barrel."

"So the gang raiding your shipments takes the stolen barrels and sells them to the ship captains," Fargo said.

"Exactly. A shipment will bring them a good price, money which we should be getting," she said.

"Why not send armed guards with your boats?"

"The Métis told us they wouldn't deliver the shipments if they were going to be caught in gun battles."

"Can't blame them for that."

"If we can catch the gang raiding our shipments, we can go after them and put an end to all of it. I'm hoping you can get a lead on this while I'm searching for my father," she said.

"I'll do my best," Fargo replied as they walked on past more of the Métis women gutting salmon. Fargo saw many wave and nod at Heather. "They seem to know you," he said.

"Why wouldn't they?" she answered.

"You said you'd been away for a few years."

"I guess they have good memories," she said. "We've other stations along the Nelson. They'll probably remember me there, too."

Fargo paused and gestured to a row of square carts, each with two large wheels and one-horse shafts, a square-framed body covered with some kind of hide. "Those carts—they're not like any I've ever seen," Fargo said.

"Métis Red River carts. They're made of wood and buffalo hide. They can hold a good lot of people and cargo. For river crossings, they just take off the wheels and the shafts, and the carts become square rafts. They're very practical."

"I'll bet," Fargo said admiringly as the night began to take over the last of the day. "Time to find a place to bed down," he said.

"Wherever you say," she murmured and rode beside him as he moved on alongside the river, finally finding a spot of land to set up camp on. He shared a strip of beef jerky with Heather and set out his bedroll. Heather was undressed and inside it first as

69

the moon's pale light filtered down through the trees. Her arms welcomed him, her body echoed the welcome. Her warm, ivory smoothness caressed his flesh. Once again, he heard her low, growling moans and felt her body surging forward and back, her every motion a study of flowing rhythm, every part of her consumed in her own growling passion.

He held her, felt his own passions escalating as she rumbled with delight, her surging body carrying him along with it. He had already come to know the feel of those soft motions and come to enjoy it as well. Her thighs tightened, pressing into him and he moved with her, feeling himself erupting with her. The wonderful joining, forever the same and forever different. Finally, she hushed down to a purring whisper and then there was only the sound of her steady breathing. She was already asleep against him, and he stayed with her, once again falling into a deep slumber as she shifted in the night to stay against his side. When morning came, she woke with him and he met her hazel eyes as they bored into him. Once more, her eyes held that satisfied light in their depths, almost a kind of victory in it.

She lay still as he swung from the bedroll. He dressed and gathered his gear as she rose and dressed, her full, lovely figure moving with a womanly grace. Finally, she was in the saddle riding beside him, leading the way north again and maintaining a parallel path to the river. He found a stand of apple trees and when they finished breakfast he saw the trees grow denser, heavy growths of northern white cedar, quaking aspen and red pine. He caught another glimpse of the river where the trees spread out for a moment. "It's widening," he said.

"It'll keep widening as we go north. It goes through Split Lake and then on to where the schooners wait just below Port Nelson and Hudson Bay. Our headquarters is just past Split Lake," Heather said and the river grew harder to glimpse as she took an elk trail that led deeper into the white cedar and aspen. They rode into the late afternoon and the forest stayed a silent, shaded place with heavy underbrush on both sides of the elk trail. Only the abrupt flight of a horned owl and ruffed grouse interrupted the stillness as they rode. Fargo's eyes peered back and forth through the trees, probing, searching, a habit as much a part of him as breathing. But suddenly he felt the Ovaro tighten under him and the horse tossed its jet-black head.

Fargo frowned as he lay a soothing hand alongside the horse's powerful neck. He stayed relaxed in the saddle but now his eyes darted deeper into the trees. Something had alarmed the horse and he had the utmost confidence in the pinto's sensitivity. This was no companion that spooked at unimportant things. Fargo's frown remained as he sought to perhaps spy a bear or some gray wolves. He was still probing through the thick leaves of the aspen and the overlapping, yellow-green branchlets of the northern white cedar when he found the horse and rider almost hidden behind a wide cedar. He moved on, spotting another horseman waiting in the trees, then another a dozen yards on.

He whispered low as he reached Heather. "Keep riding just as you are. Don't look around. We've got company."

He saw the frown dig into her brow. "You sure?" she asked.

"Very sure," he muttered. "I'd guess at least a half dozen. They've been waiting in the trees."

"Damn," she bit out. "Can we run?"

"No. The best we can do is get a jump on them. Get ready to ride hard when I tell you to," he said and saw her gather her reins in, her body stiffening in preparation. He held their leisurely pace for another dozen yards when he glimpsed two more half-hidden horsemen and saw one start to send his horse forward. "Now," he rasped. *"Ride!"* Putting the Ovaro into an instant gallop, he sent the horse racing from the elk trail into the thickest of the aspen and white cedar with Heather at his heels, and set a swerving path. He heard the sound of the hiding horsemen as they put their horses into motion. But he had a thirty-second head start. It would have to be enough.

Swerving through a dense cluster of cedar, he lifted himself in the stirrups as he threw commands back at Heather. "Jump! Don't pull on your horse, let him go!" he shouted as he leaped from the saddle. He hit the ground and crashed into the underbrush and the pinto raced on. From behind he heard Heather landing inches from him. Reaching out, he found her arm and pulled her along as he sank into the tall underbrush. The Colt was in his hand as he whirled, and the horsemen raced past, following the sound of the Ovaro and the grey galloping ahead through the forest. They'd catch up to the two riderless horses in moments, realize that they'd been tricked and come charging back to hunt down their quarry. Then they'd have the hunter's advantage plus the advantage of numbers.

Fargo knew his only chance was to cut down that advantage, and as the riders flew past he counted off five of them, then raised the Colt and drew a bead on the last three. The Colt exploded, moved a fraction with each as he got off three shots. Two of the figures stiffened in the saddle and flung their arms out sideways as they toppled from their horses. The third one buckled almost in two as he fell forward from his mount and plunged to the ground. Fargo heard the other two shout as they reined up, peeled off and turned to come back. Now they moved carefully, slowly edging their way through the aspen and cedars, pausing every few steps to listen.

Fargo stayed in the high brush. Heather flattened beside him, concern but no fear in her face. A faint rustle of leaves caught his ear and he let a grim smile touch his lips. The two men tried to move quietly, but they were neither hunters nor trappers. They hadn't trained their bodies to respond to their efforts, hadn't spent the years needed to master the art of making will and action the same. Their steps more stiff than silent, they moved carefully, unaware that the man they faced picked up every susurrant sound and every rustling blade of grass. Fargo waited, hardly breathing, his ears telling him that one of the two men moved left, the other right. He chose the one at the left, gesturing again for Heather to stay motionless and moving forward on sliding steps that let him move through the underbrush without a sound.

He followed the noise of the man in front of him, whose figure came into sight as he moved between trees. The man took long, awkward steps in an effort to be stealthy, and Fargo slid a few paces closer. He leaned against the fibrous, reddish-brown bark of a cedar. "Drop the gun," he said in a low whisper only the figure in front of him could hear. "Do it." The man stiffened, and turned to the sound of Fargo's whispered voice. Then, with the predictableness inherent in human nature, he snapped his gun up to fire. Fargo's Colt barked first, a single shot that hurled the man backwards as his chest spurted scarlet.

Fargo dropped to the ground at once as the sound of the shot died away. Fargo expected a flurry of gunfire from the other man but there was only silence. Fargo almost smiled. The man was unsure what the single shot meant. Muffling the tone of his voice with his hand over his mouth, Fargo called out, "Over here," as he stayed low, peering through the tall brush. The last man appeared moments later, coming in from the right, moving through the trees and on toward him.

"Harry?" he called.

Fargo let him draw a few steps closer before pushing to his feet. "It's not Harry," he said. "Don't be as dumb as Harry." He watched the man peer through the trees for the origin of the voice, the six-gun in his hand. "I get answers. You stay alive," Fargo said.

The man hesitated, then growled, "Don't have any answers."

"Try again," Fargo said and heard Heather pull herself out of the brush.

"We got paid to watch for her," the man said, nodding at Heather.

"Just watch for her?" Fargo queried.

"Take her. Kill her if we had to," he said.

"Who paid you?" Fargo asked.

"Never gave a name."

"Where were you supposed to take her?"

"We was just supposed to hold on to her," the man said.

74

Heather's voice cut in. "You won't get any answers from him. Stop wasting time," she snapped.

Fargo saw the alarm leap in the man's eyes. "That's all I know. Honest," he said.

"He's lying. Kill him," Heather ordered. Fargo saw the alarm in the man's eyes change to panic, and spotted the man pulling his six-gun up to fire. Fargo grimaced as he knew there was no time to do anything but fire. His finger tightened on the trigger, and the man shuddered as the Colt barked. He managed to get off one wild shot as he fell backward and lay still.

"Dammit," Fargo snapped at her. "Maybe I could've gotten more out of him. You set him off."

"He wouldn't talk," she said dismissively. "It'd have ended the same way. We couldn't let him run back and report."

"If I'd gotten him to talk he'd have run off on his own. He wouldn't dare go back to his bosses," Fargo said.

"It's done. No point in crying over spilled milk," she said coldly.

"Let's get the horses," Fargo said, not certain if he was more annoyed at her interference or at her not having learned anything. She followed as he strode through the forest until he slowed and gave a low whistle. The Ovaro took only minutes to return and Heather rode in the saddle in front of him as they went on to search for the grey. They found it grazing on a bed of snowberries and she transferred over to her horse, riding beside him as the forest began to thin. Open land spread out beyond with small knots of red pine and stunted aspen. "Somebody doesn't want you to come visit," he said as he nosed the pinto into open land.

"We knew that after the first attack back in Lakeshore," Heather said.

"But this nails it down. How do they know you're coming back?"

"Maybe somebody saw me and told them," Heather said.

"Them being people inside your pa's company," Fargo said, and she nodded.

"Has to be, I think," she said. "Maybe Sam Simpson told them. Maybe that's where he rushed off to in such a hurry after I showed up."

Fargo's lips pursed in thought. Simpson had met up with someone. The prints had shown that. Had Simpson delivered his message and then been silenced? Fargo wondered at the thought and knew he had never been satisfied with Monique's explanation of a highwayman robbery. The question would stay just that until he could learn more. He followed Heather as she rode closer to where he could see the river again. It had widened considerably, he noted as they rode into the late afternoon, edging the small knots of pine and aspen.

He glimpsed another work post in the distance at the river's shore, where the Métis worked alongside the long tables and barrels. Most of the canoes and dugouts were already loaded with salmon-filled barrels of brine, and among the canoes on shore he saw two one-man kayaks. Heather slowed as they passed the station. "This is our last work station before the Nelson flows through Split Lake and then really widens. It's the last good place to raid the barrels," she said. "I want you to stay here, find a place to hide and watch. If there's a raid, maybe you can break it up. I think they'll run if they're surprised. The damn Métis don't fight back. They just run or stand by."

"Can't blame them. They're getting paid to gut salmon, not risk their necks in gunfights," Fargo said.

"They're getting paid. That ought to be enough for them to put up a fight," Heather snapped back.

"You want me to keep watch on things here? Where will you be?" Fargo asked her.

"Going to find Daddy," she said. "I'm heading on to our headquarters north of Split Lake."

"Alone?" He frowned. "That doesn't seem too smart."

"I'll handle whatever comes up."

"That's big talk," he said.

"You keep watch on the post for three days. If nothing happens you come get me at headquarters. How's that?" she said.

"Still not my idea of a good move," he told her.

"There are people I can talk to better if I'm alone," she said. "I have my ways. I can be very persuasive."

"I've come to know that," he conceded and she let a tiny, sly little smile edge her lush lips.

Darkness suddenly began to roll over them. "Find a place to bed down," she said. The night settled in after he led the way into a small stand of white cedar. After he unsaddled the horses, Heather produced two strips of dried beef, which they shared.

"We'll have to restock soon," Fargo said.

"We can do that at headquarters," she said as he set out his bedroll. Once again, she was the first to get inside it, her naked loveliness encompassing him. Her eagerness took only moments to inflame, delight and arouse, and he moved with the rhythm of her slow surgings and the low moans that throbbed up from deep inside her.

"You're getting to be a habit," he murmured. "And a damn nice one." Her answer was to increase the undulating motions of her long body until that moment came again as she moaned and pushed until finally she lay spent in his arms. He slept with her until the night passed and the sun wound its way through the trees. He let her dress first, enjoying the beauty of it, and finally he was standing with her beside the grey. "Still don't like you going on alone," he said.

"I'll find out more that way. I know exactly what I'm doing," she said.

"Three days and I come after you," he said.

"Just follow the river past Split Lake and you'll come to it," she said, swinging into the saddle and riding off. He let the sound of the grey's hoofbeats fade away before he took the Ovaro and rode toward the river, not slowing until he drew closer to the work station. He found a thin line of red pine and turned into the trees that provided cover, letting him see the work station. He dismounted, got down low and prepared to wait, his eyes sweeping the work station and the Métis still hard at work.

By the end of the day, only a dozen or so barrels were left to fill, and as night came, the Métis trudged off toward a long, bunkhouse-like shack in the distance. Fargo rose, stretched his legs and finished another of the few remaining strips of beef jerky. He slept, half awake with his ears tuned in to pick up any unusual sounds. But the night was still and he woke with the new day, and commenced watching the Métis again as they returned and began filling the last dozen barrels. When the sun passed the noon mark, he saw the men begin to load the final capped barrels onto the last of the dugouts. They were almost finished when Fargo felt a rumble coming through the ground, then heard the thunder of hoofbeats. He saw the Métis catch the sound, alarm shooting through them at once in the way they stared into the distance as if frozen in place.

The horses came into sight moments later, at least a dozen riders, all holding rifles. They raced to the work station and drew to a halt in a half circle with their rifles raised. Fargo saw the Métis shrink back and cluster together. "Very smart," one of the riders said. "Keep going, get out of here." The Métis continued their retreat, turning and hurrying toward the long bunkhouse shack in the distance. They were plainly not about to put up a battle. Nor was he, Fargo decided. Not at this time. He needed a better place to take on those odds. He'd wait and pick his spot before going into action. He settled down to watch but a frown dug into his brow.

Ten of the riders dismounted and began climbing into the dugouts and the canoes while the other two men saw to the horses, looping reins together. Those in the boats began to paddle away, and Fargo guessed it would take them at least two days, perhaps more, to reach where the schooners waited. But his frown creased deeper when the men didn't paddle north. Instead, they turned south, moving downriver. They had made their raid, taken what they wanted. Why weren't they going on up the Nelson to the waiting schooners to sell their stolen goods? He watched them go on rowing south and knew he could do only one thing—follow. But that could be damn near impossible, he grimaced. They were moving in daylight in wide open spaces. If he got close enough to see he'd be spotted for sure. "Shit," he swore as they rowed on around a slow curve. As the two riders left behind began to move off, pulling the other ten horses with them, Fargo tethered the Ovaro in the trees and began to run toward the two kayaks that had been left behind.

He pushed one into the water and climbed into the opening in the center of the boat. It was a tight fit, but he managed to wedge his big frame into the boat and, using the double-ended paddle, moved into the middle of the river. Paddling slowly and silently, he sailed downriver after the others, who were now out of sight. He held a steady pace, trying to pick up the sound of their boats pushing through the water, but that proved impossible, and he didn't dare try to catch up. Being seen was too risky. He held to his pace, and steered to row along the edge of the shoreline under growths of Bebb Willows.

The day was sliding toward an end as the river made a sharp turn right. He started around it, cursing silently as he backpaddled to a halt. The canoes and dugouts were halted against the shore at the end of the curve. He steered the kayak onto the riverbank, got out and pulled the little craft partially up on the shore. Flattening himself on a field of burdock, the plants not much over two feet high, he began to crawl forward, pausing to peer through the oval leaves of the weeds. A wagon, closed at the sides not unlike a bakery wagon, had been rolled almost to the water's edge. Most of the barrels had been unloaded onto the shore. He saw five more men who had plainly come with the wagon, and as the other men moved barrels to the rear of the wagon, six others took up positions as guards, each holding a rifle. Fargo lay motionless. Hew as only able to partially view the wagon and the men bringing barrels to the rear of it. Night began to roll across the land, blanketing the scene quickly, and Fargo raised his head and peered into the darkness. As he did, a leap of flame stabbed through the night.

They had built a fire, one just large enough to light whatever they were doing but not enough to let him discern anything. The guards were still in position, he saw. He began to crawl forward, inching his way closer to the scene as he watched. He saw most of the men move from the wagon and settle down on the ground with blankets and bedrolls. They were asleep in minutes and soon Fargo saw the guards join the others in sleep. He continued to inch his way along the ground. The fire quickly burned low, leaving just enough light to cast a soft glow across the barrels. Rising, he moved forward on steps soft as a panther on the prowl, circling the barrels. He moved from one to the other, each with its lid in place and drew the slender throwing knife from its holster around his ankle.

Using the tip of the blade, he began to pry the lid from one of the barrels, working ever so carefully, very aware that any noise would bring a hail of gunfire from all around him. Finally, he loosened the lid enough to lift it from the barrel, and he stared down into the brine-filled container. Salmon, stacked together on their ends, their heads staring up at him, completely filled the barrel. Again working very slowly and silently, he replaced the lid and went on to the next barrel. Prying that lid off, he found himself again staring down at a barrel filled with salmon. He went on to the one beside it, then the next, slowly and methodically prying the lids from each barrel. Nothing but salmon greeted him as he moved from barrel to barrel.

The frown deepened on his brow as he carefully replaced the lid on another barrel. Questions circled like hawks inside his mind. Things didn't fit. They plainly weren't replacing the salmon with other things they wanted to smuggle past the inspectors. But then why hadn't they gone north to the schooners? Why had they come all the way back here to meet a waiting wagon? There had to be a reason. He was missing something but he had no idea what. Fargo started to turn away but his mind was still wrestling with the stabbing, unresolved questions, his attention distracted. His foot struck against one of the barrels. It moved with a sudden, scraping sound that seemed loud as a revolver shot.

Fargo's eyes leaped to the figures all around him, saw them snapping awake, pushing to their feet as they drew their guns. In seconds, they'd be pouring lead into him from all directions. He flung himself forward in a diving leap, knocking aside two more of the barrels and hitting the ground rolling. The first volley of shots thudded into the dirt just behind him as the last of the fire went out. He kept rolling as another volley of wild shots kicked up soil. But he had reached the river and he flung himself into the water with a loud splash. Instantly, another barrage erupted, shots tearing through the water. Fargo sank under the surface and swam underwater, feeling the thudding of bullets that ploughed through the water on all sides of him.

He dove down, felt his feet touch the bottom of the

river and half swam, half crawled until his lungs seemed on fire and about to burst. He used the last of his strength to propel himself upwards. But he had neither breath nor time to surface quietly, and he burst into the air gulping in deep draughts with a hoarse sound. His attackers heard him at once, and immediately unleashed another barrage even though the firelight was gone and they could only throw lead in the direction of the sound. But they were running toward him as they fired, and he took another deep breath and dove again. Wild barrages could kill as thoroughly as aimed ones, he knew, as he kicked out for the bottom of the river. But this time he changed direction as he swam underwater until his lungs threatened to burst again.

When he came up, he was behind where the men moved along the shore searching for any sight or sound of him. A quarter moon had come up to cast a faint light as he swam to the shore upriver from the searchers. Crawling onto the riverbank, he moved inland away from the river and turned south only when he felt he was far enough away not to be seen. He fell into a loping run, and he could hear the men as he passed behind them. They were lined up on the shore, looking and listening for any sign of him, wondering if their shots had taken him down. He kept at his ground-eating pace and turned to the river only when he had gone at least another hundred yards.

He made his way back to the shore, running south along it until he found the kayak where he had left it. Silently, he slid the craft into the water and paddled back to the station. He left the kayak and retrieved the Ovaro in the red pines and rode. The moon told him there were a few hours of night left and he found another cluster of aspen and pushed into its center. He set out his bedroll and felt exhaustion pull at him. Plans and unanswered questions would keep until the morning as he let sleep slide over him.

5

When morning came he rode to the river, let the Ovaro drink, then washed. When he was in the saddle again he turned north, hugging the riverbank. When he came onto long growths of Bebb Willows he stayed in the cover of their dull-green, elliptical leaves, which hung low to the ground. At a particularly heavy growth of willows, he halted and moved back deep into the trees and settled down to wait. His eyes scanned the river and soon he saw a handful of trappers and hunters paddle downriver in canoes, all moving alone with their pelts. The sun had moved into the noon hour and the raiders didn't appear, though he continued to squint upriver for any sign of them.

They were plainly in no hurry to bring their stolen catch to the schooners. Perhaps they waited to be joined by those from another raid. That made a certain amount of sense, he pondered. One large, simple deal instead of a number of small ones. But that was the only thing that made any sense. It was time to go to Heather, tell her what he had seen and see if she had any explanations. He left the protection of the willows and sent the Ovaro forward, following the river as it ran a fairly straight line north, widening as it progressed. The day had slid into midafternoon when he reached Split Lake and found a large river flowing from the lake, turning to the northeast. Fargo pressed on.

The day was beginning to near an end when a cluster of wooden buildings came into view. He counted six, of various sizes, all near the river's edge. The largest had a second story, and as he drew closer he saw the sign hanging over the door: Grandy Trading Company. There were no long tables nor rows of barrels as there were at the other work stations, but two wooden piers stretched alongside the river. A half-dozen men moved among the buildings, most carrying one thing or another, and Fargo saw a flat raft tied to one of the piers. He rode on to the largest of the buildings, dismounted and went inside. He found a large, cavernous interior with boxes and crates stacked all around in a jumbled fashion. He saw fishing gear, trapping and hunting equipment. One corner was filled with tent poles, another with boxes of dry rations. He also saw sleds and snowshoes stacked against each other in another corner. A stairway rising in the center of the huge room led to the floor above.

A man, of medium build with steel-grey hair on a youthful face, turned to him from beside a table covered with barrel staves. Fargo saw his piercing blue eyes take him in. "Yes?" the man said coldly.

"Looking for somebody," Fargo said. "Heather Grandy."

The man's steel-blue eyes stayed on him, a blank expression on the man's square face. "Who's looking for her?" he asked slowly.

"Name's Fargo . . . Skye Fargo."

The man's expression softened. "Oh—Heather told us you might show. I'm Rory Dermott."

"Thought Heather said you were at the north Sipi-wesk station," Fargo said.

"I move around to one place or another," Dermott said. "I'll get Heather." He turned and started up the stairway to the second floor. Fargo busied himself looking at the variety of equipment in the large room until he heard footsteps on the stairs. He turned to see Heather coming down, a shaft of the day's last sun beams shone through a window catching the auburn in her hair. She wore dark green riding britches and a light-green shirt that clung to her curvaceous figure.

"Hello," she said with a wide smile. "Didn't expect you for another day."

"Glad to see you're all right," Fargo said. "We have to talk. I've things to tell you."

"Not here," she said, reaching the floor and coming to him.

He pressed his mouth to her lips, feeling her respond. "You find out anything? Is your pa here?" he asked when they broke apart.

"No to both," she answered.

"Anybody know where he went?"

"Seems not. I guess he just took off," Heather said.

"But you told me you've never bought that story. You change your mind?" Fargo asked.

"No," she said. "But no more talk here. I'll have Rory show you to one of the guest shacks. I'll come visit you later."

"Not just to talk, I hope. I told you, you've become habit forming," he said.

Her hazel eyes roamed up and down his body. "Wouldn't want you to change a habit, especially when you've things to tell me," Heather breathed, then kissed him, stepping back as Rory Dermott came down the stairs. "Show Fargo to the second guest shack," she told Dermott, her hand lightly yet possessively touching his arm.

"This way," Rory said, and Fargo went outside into the new night, taking the Ovaro and following him to a small shack with an overhang extending from one side to keep his horse out of the elements. Rory Dermott lit a large candle in the room and the light immediately revealed a neat room with a bed, a small dresser, a chair, and a wooden basin atop the dresser. A wood-burning stove filled one corner, no doubt a necessity once the harsh winter touched the northlands. "Heather told us she hired you as a bodyguard," Dermott said.

"That's right," Fargo nodded. Heather had plainly decided on revealing less than the truth.

"You do a lot of that back in the States?" the man questioned.

"Enough," Fargo said blandly.

"You need anything, come to the main office," Dermott offered and hurried from the shack. The big candle provided not only light but warmth, and after unsaddling the Ovaro, Fargo tested the bed in the shack, finding it not too uncomfortable. He was stretched out, dozing, when he heard the door open, and he sat up as Heather entered. She sat down beside him, her eyes again appreciatively studying his rugged face.

"Every time I see you I think how handsome you are," she said, pressing her lips to his, letting their warm wetness linger for a long moment before drawing back.

"You stopping?" he asked.

"I want to hear what you have to tell me," she said.

"There was a raid. As you said would happen, the Métis didn't resist," he said, sitting back. He went on to recount how he had followed the raiders south, telling her everything else that had happened. "You have any take on it?" he asked when he finished.

"Maybe your guess was right," Heather shrugged. "Maybe they're waiting. Maybe they want to get more than the results of one raid."

"My guess seems right, but I'm not happy with it," Fargo said.

"Why not?"

"Why'd they bring the barrels out of the canoes and bring them to the rear of the wagon? They could've left them in the canoes while they waited."

Her lips pursed as she thought for a moment. "A sudden thunderstorm can easily tip over canoes and swamp dugouts. Maybe that's what they were afraid of."

Fargo frowned. "Maybe, but their kind doesn't usually think that far ahead."

"You've anything better?" she asked.

"No," he admitted. "But let's get back to you. Why'd you tell them I was going to arrive here?"

She took a moment to answer. "They didn't believe I'd come alone. They kept pressing me. I thought it best to tell them something."

"So you came up with me being a bodyguard."

"Anything wrong with that?" she questioned.

"You didn't want to tell them you'd hired me to find your pa. You could've just said I was a friend."

"A special friend," she said, the little smile coming back to her lips.

"Why not? Give them a little truth," he said and pulled her to him, finding the warmth of her full lips.

"Why not?" she echoed, breaking away for a moment. "Bed and truth. They go together." She kissed him again. Her tongue darted forward, caressing, a sweet message, and as they kissed he took off his holster, tossed it on the floor and followed it with the rest of his clothes. In moments, she was naked against him, pressing her ivory-skinned softness into him. She rose, brought her full, pear-shaped breasts to his face, and let his mouth draw in one, then the other. Swinging her legs around, she came over him, reached for his throbbing, seeking erectness and slowly slid forward. Sweet, wet walls embraced him, surrounded him, encompassed him with excruciating pleasure. Heather moved farther forward, her legs straddling him, pressing down to take in all of his throbbing answer to her desire. She began to move up and down, a motion that quickly became wild, bucking, twisting, urgent ride to ecstacy.

She bucked harder, higher, slamming down onto him and bucking again, and her full breasts bounced in rhythm. "Oh, yes, yes, yes," Heather gasped, little high-pitched sounds that quickly became screams, each cry rising higher, gathering new strength. Her hair flew from side to side and became a tempest-tossed auburn mane as every part of her writhed and bucked, rose and fell, turned and twisted, her wild screams filling the little shack. "Oh, God, oh my God, yes, yes, yes!" she managed to say between screams as she continued to buck with frantic motions, each an exercise in ecstacy, when suddenly he saw her eyes widen and felt her body stiffen.

With a shrieking, piercing scream, she stayed as if

frozen in place atop him for a long, breathless second and then she fell forward over him, staying pressed tight against him as she quivered and shook. Little high-pitched cries of pleasure fell from lips that danced against his chest. He felt his own pleasure explode with her maelstrom of passion, and the world seemed to fade away, gradually returning after seconds that seemed timeless. With a final scream she went limp. She lay over him, unmoving, and he wondered if she had fainted. He held her and then, with a sigh that was more a cry, she slid from him to lie heavily against him, one leg over his groin. He remained motionless, holding her, until she stirred, drew her leg down and pushed upwards. He rose on his elbows to see her half-lidded eyes peering at him.

"That was something special," he said, his gaze moving across her lush body before returning to her eyes. "Who are you?" he asked.

Her eyes came fully open instantly. "What?" She frowned.

"Who are you?" he repeated.

She sat up straighter. "What kind of a question is that?" she snapped. "I'm Heather."

Slowly, he ran his hands through her auburn hair, across her face, her breasts, down to her thighs, pressing into the denseness of her venus mound. "No, you're not," he said evenly. "You're exactly like her, same hair, same eyes, same lips, same breasts, same deep-pink nipples, same auburn-tinted nap—the same in every way except one."

"Have you gone crazy?" she snapped.

"No, not crazy," Fargo said as he studied her. Suddenly he felt the rush of realization sweep through him. "You're a twin, by God, a damn twin! That's it, an identical twin, except for one thing."

"What are you talking about?" She frowned.

"Maybe it's the one thing that never could be the same," he said. "You look the same, feel the same, sound the same, but you fuck differently. You don't moan the same, don't move the same, don't come the same. That's where you're different. 'By their orgasms ye shall know them.' Book of Fargo." She stared back at him and he saw the coating of ice form over her hazel eyes. "And you'd have pulled it off except for that one difference. That's something you never thought about. But *why*?" he said.

She turned, remaining silent for a moment, then took him by surprise by flinging herself from the bed, diving to reach his gun in the holster on the floor. He caught her by the legs just as her fingers grasped for the gun, pulled her back and flung her onto the bed. Her breasts bounced as she landed, and she spun around to face him, her eyes boring into him. "No dice, honey," he growled. "Talk, twin sister. Start with your name."

"Hallie," she bit out.

"Where's Heather?" he demanded.

"Safe," she said.

"Not good enough," he said.

"It'll have to do," she threw back.

He closed one hand around her neck. "Try again. I'm not here to play games," he said.

Her lips tightened, but he saw the dark shadow of fear touch her eyes. "She's in one of our cabins," Hallie said.

"Why'd you come on as Heather?" he asked.

"I wanted to find out more about you," she said.

"And you had to go all the way to carry it off," he laughed.

"You would've gotten suspicious if I didn't," she said.

"And you might've pulled it off except for that one thing," he said. She glared at him. "But you stopped acting and began enjoying it," he added.

"Go to hell," she flung at him, and he laughed again. "May I get dressed?" she asked.

"Sure, if you want to," he returned. She refused to answer and he reached down, tossed her clothes to her and began to pull on his own things. "Let's get back to Heather. How come she told you about me?" he queried.

"We got it out of her," Hallie said.

"Not just by asking, I'll bet," Fargo grunted, and once again she didn't answer. "Where's your father? That's why she came. She was afraid for him. She says he's in danger."

"Is that what she told you?"

"You saying different?" he questioned.

"Oh, he's in danger, all right. He's in danger from Heather. That's why he ran away," she said.

Fargo felt a frown tug at his brow. "I don't like riddles," he growled.

Hallie Grandy finished buttoning up her blouse and turned to face him. "My sister is mad, as in insane," she said flatly. "She enjoys killing people, especially men. Heather has killed several men. She doesn't need much of a reason, anything that annoys her is justification enough. She's also killed a few women. Killing is a hobby with her."

Fargo's eyes drilled into Hallie Grandy. "That's a hell of an accusation."

"It took the authorities a long time to catch on to her. Only when they started investigating, looking back at the facts, did they begin to make connections. They kept digging until they put all the pieces together."

Fargo stared at Hallie and felt as though he'd been flung into a whirlpool. Her words were too monstrous to simply accept. Yet one picture kept surfacing in the sea of swirling thoughts inside him. He kept seeing a derringer, a Remington, a man dead on a hotel room floor and an explanation that had always nagged at him. Now its glib cleverness stabbed at him again and he brought his eyes back to Hallie. "You're asking more than I'm prepared to believe just on your word," he said.

"I suppose so," Hallie said. "Where'd she tell you she's been the last few years?"

"Traveling," he said.

"She's been under lock and key in the Manitoba Asylum for the Criminally Insane," Hallie said.

MACI. Fargo felt as though he'd suddenly been kicked in the stomach. Another night rose up in his memory, the night he had caught the man who'd been trailing Heather. Heather had killed him with two shots from her little four-barrelled derringer. The card he'd found on the man identified him as a special officer for MACI, enigmatic initials Hallie had given a new and chilling meaning. But he'd not let words and memories run away with him, he told himself. "I still want to see her and talk to her," he said. "Take me to her."

Her eyes speared him. "You take a lot of convincing," Hallie said.

94

"That's right. If Heather is everything you say, how come she's here?" Fargo tossed at her.

"She escaped. She's very clever. The asylum sent word to us. That's when Father decided to run. Heather has always blamed him for not fighting the authorities, for letting them put her away. She's told him she'd never forget it and that she'd pay him back for it. When we learned she'd escaped, he knew she'd be coming back for him. He hoped that by running, he'd keep her chasing after him, leaving the rest of us alone. He was afraid for all of us."

He peered at her. She had given him words and images, evoked things he couldn't ignore, yet it was still all words, and words could be twisted, used as weapons. Hallie used more than words to pursue what she wanted. She'd proven that. "I still want to see Heather. Take me to her," he said.

"No," Hallie said.

"We can do this the hard way if we have to," he told her. "What are you afraid of?" he questioned.

"Heather is very clever, extremely persuasive. It took four sheriffs from different towns to catch on to her. She might convince you I'm making this up. It wouldn't surprise me," Hallie said.

"Not likely. There are things I want her to explain away," Fargo said. "Besides, too many things still don't add up with you."

"Such as?"

"Your salmon trade is being raided, ruined. You haven't even mentioned that. Heather knew about it so you must know, too," he pushed at her.

"Heather knows because she got regular reports. That was part of the terms of her sentence. She has a stake in the company," Hallie answered.

"That doesn't explain your silence about it," he said.

"It's our problem. I don't talk about our problems with strangers. Besides, it's got nothing to do with this," Hallie said.

"Take me to Heather. Last chance," he said, his voice finding an edge.

"She's under guard and I've men all over. You can't get her out," Hallie said.

"Didn't say I would," he returned.

"I can't take that chance," she said. "You should believe me, Fargo, about everything."

"I don't know what I should believe. That's why I'm going to see Heather. Try and stop me and people will get hurt. You could be one of them," he said.

She studied him for a moment and he saw a tiny smugness slide across her face. "You're not the kind to shoot a girl you just slept with," she murmured.

"You're right. But I thought I was sleeping with Heather, remember? Until orgasm time. That means you don't really count."

"Damn you," she threw at him and her hand came out to smash against his face but he drew back and her blow sailed wide.

"Not quick enough, honey, another place," he said.

"To hell with you," she snapped.

"Talking's over," he said with sudden harshness, as he started to draw the Colt.

"I need a promise," Hallie said, her tone softening.

"What kind of a promise?"

"I'll take you to her if you promise you won't try to get her out until we talk again," she said.

He turned the offer over in his mind, and decided he could do with it. Besides, he wanted to avoid a

96

shootout. "Deal," he said. She nodded and turned, and he followed her from the shack. She led the way to another shack where four men with rifles stood guard. He sized them up in one quick glance. He'd be able to take the four of them if he had to, he decided as Hallie halted before the shack and the guards parted for her. She turned to Fargo.

"Your gun," she said.

"We made a deal," he said.

"We did," she said. "All right, go on in."

"I like a woman who keeps her word," he said as he opened the door of the shack and went in. A kerosene lamp lit up the interior and Heather jumped up from a cot and ran to him, flinging her arms around him.

"Oh, God, you're here! I was waiting, hoping," she said, and Fargo had to remind himself he was not holding Hallie despite the bruise on her cheekbone. She pressed her lips to his, finally drawing back.

"Coming here alone didn't work out," he said, and she gave an offhanded shrug. "You never said you had a twin sister."

"Didn't seem important," she said.

"That's interesting," he said. "You've more things to tell me that didn't seem important?"

She let her full lips form a pout. "I know what Hallie's told you," she sniffed.

"Is she lying?" he questioned.

"You don't believe her, do you?" Heather frowned.

"I'm not believing anything yet but a lot of things don't add up," he said.

"Such as?"

"Ernie Binder. Your story about self-defense never sat right with me."

"Why not?"

"Too clever. What you did took planning. Then there was Sam Simpson. He was really upset to see you appear and soon after he raced away. Monique wondered why. So did I. Maybe you didn't," Fargo said.

"Go on. I'm fascinated," she said, her voice grown chilly.

"He met a lone rider and was killed. You'd gone off yourself that night. Did you wait for him, stop him from coming here to tell them you'd come back?" Fargo asked.

"Of course not," she said, but her disdain had a glib, hollow ring to it, and he peered sharply at her.

"Then there was that lawman you shot dead before I could question him. I found out what those initials on his identity card meant. You said you didn't know," he reminded her.

"I forgot," she said, no anger or protest in her voice, only an eerie dismissal, as if it were all beneath discussing.

"You forgot what they meant? That's hard to believe, you living in Manitoba," Fargo said. She shrugged again, her hazel eyes masked, and he felt the sinking feeling grow in the pit of his stomach. He had to reach her, shatter that cloak she'd drawn around herself. "I can find out if you forgot," he said.

"How?" she returned calmly.

"Suppose I take you back to MACI. If they don't know you at the asylum you're in the clear," Fargo said.

She whirled toward him, her voice suddenly a strained shout. "No!" she said, the cords in her neck standing out, her face growing red with fear and fury.

"No, damn you! I don't have to prove anything to you!" Fargo grimaced. Her contained mask had torn open and too many things took on new meanings as they fell into place. "I hired you to help me find my father. Nothing's changed about that," she said.

"I wouldn't exactly say that," Fargo muttered wryly.

"You're actually going to believe Hallie?" Heather frowned.

"It's not Hallie. It's you and all the things that add up now, all the smooth explanations you had for shooting too many, too fast."

"All because I won't go visit the asylum with you?"

"There's always a last straw," he said, turned and strode to the door, a sour taste in his mouth.

"You'll be sorry for this," Heather called.

"I'm already sorry," he said, his hand pausing on the doorknob. Hallie waited with the four men, he was certain. He'd try to make Hallie cooperate with him. He pulled the door open, stepped out and saw a dozen rifles pointed at him, Hallie standing to one side.

"I figured four men wouldn't be enough for you," she said.

"I'm complimented, but we had a deal. We need to talk some more," he said.

"No we don't. We'll be doing things my way," she said and gestured to one of the riflemen. "Take his gun." Fargo eyed the array of rifles again and cursed silently. To try a shootout would be suicide. The man lifted the Colt from his holster and stepped back with the others. "Put him in the guard shack," Hallie said.

"What are you going to do with Heather?" he asked.

"We'll take care of her," Hallie said.

"I believe what you told me. Let's work this out," he tried.

"I don't need you to work things out," Hallie said with the same iciness he had seen Heather summon and he stared at her for a long moment.

"Twins, except for one thing," he reminded her.

Her eyes narrowed. "Take him away," she barked, and the riflemen lined up around him and began to march him away. He walked with thoughts cascading through his mind, his last words to Hallie clinging to him. Perhaps they'd been too right, he muttered as they reached the shack, the guards opening the door and throwing him inside. He landed on a wood floor in a room with a single candle burning inside that revealed a narrow cot and one barred window. Was this to be his last place in this world? It was all too possible, he realized.

6

By stretching, Fargo found he could peer out the lone window, just in time to see Hallie's riflemen trudging away from the shack. All but two had left, he counted. Hallie obviously felt confident two were enough to guard an unarmed man for the night. It was a mistake others had made before her, he thought as he reached down to the thin leather holster around his ankle and pulled out the slender Arkansas toothpick. Returning to the door, he curled one hand around the knob, slowly moving it back and forth. It instantly made a harsh scraping sound, and he drew his hand back at once, swearing softly.

It was an old, rusted mechanism, the bolt, tumblers, cam and ward worn and jagged. Even a new lock in smooth, good condition would take the utmost care to pry open silently. This one would be impossible. Two guards standing sentry right outside with nothing to do but look and listen would be certain to hear the rusted mechanism as he worked on it. They'd realize he had something with him and the last thing he wanted was to have his remaining weapon taken. He drew back, returned the slender blade to its ankle holster and went to the cot and stretched out. He had long ago learned the art of waiting, and in this case, he had no choice. He let sleep come to him.

The morning sun sifting itself through the bars woke him. He found a pitcher of water in the shack and washed. A hole in the ground at the rear of the room served as a latrine. He lay down again, his mind wrestling with possibilities for escape as he realized they were damn few. It was mid morning when he heard the commotion at the door and he swung from the cot and stood up. Four riflemen entered first, then Hallie. She, in turn, was followed by a big man, taller than Fargo, with a strong, hawklike face. Fargo had only to see his deep-red hair and hazel eyes to know who he was.

"Well, well. Family reunion?" Fargo remarked.

"You could say that," Hallie answered. "I sent for my father as soon as we had Heather under lock and key. It took him till now to get back."

Fargo saw Rupert Grandy size him up with a piercing stare. "Too bad for you, mister American," Grandy said. "You took up with the wrong woman."

"Not the first time," Fargo shrugged. "You going to take her back to the asylum?" He saw Rupert Grandy exchange glances with Hallie.

"No," Hallie answered. "We won't be doing that."

Fargo's eyes narrowed, the unsaid hanging in Hallie's answer. "You want to spell that out?" he queried.

"Heather's been nothing but trouble. It's time to put an end to it," Grandy said harshly.

"If she's insane, taking her back is the right thing to do," Fargo said.

"She escaped once. She could escape again. We won't risk that," the man said.

"I don't believe what I'm hearing. Your own

daughter?" Fargo said to Grandy, then turned his eyes to Hallie. "Your own sister?"

Hallie shrugged. "She's our problem. We'll take care of it our way."

Fargo returned his eyes to Rupert Grandy. "The asylum already sent one man out after her. They'll send another. They'll keep looking. Sooner or later they'll come asking you hard questions."

"We've thought about that problem, but it's one you've solved for us," Grandy said.

"Me?" Fargo frowned.

"You'll supply the piece we need to make it all come out right," Grandy said. "With Heather's record of killing her men friends, she's going to kill you. Only you'll have managed to get off one shot."

"That kills her," Fargo said.

"Exactly. It'll all fit in with her history, a nice, neat package. Nobody will question it for a moment," Grandy said.

"We'll use a derringer to kill you. Heather liked to use derringers. Then after you're dead, we'll go get your Colt from the office, and we'll kill her with it. After that it's just careful placing of the right weapons in the right hands and it's done," Hallie said.

Fargo stared at Grandy. The scheme was neat, all right. It would be swallowed easily. But there was something more behind it. They were afraid of more than just Heather escaping the asylum again. "You're some pair," he bit out.

"I'll take that as a compliment," the man sneered.

"Don't," Fargo said.

"But there's one bit of good news for you. We can't get at this for another day. We've other things to tend to," Grandy said. "You've a little more time to contemplate your past and your future." He laughed and strode from the shack and Fargo's eyes went to Hallie.

"Excuse me if I don't say thank you," he said and she shrugged. "I've a going away present for you. You can't forget the other night."

She looked thoughtfully at him. "That's true," she said. "But some things just don't work out right."

"This could," he tried.

She glanced at him with almost sadness. "No. Heather's too insane and you're too smart," she said, then turned and hurried from the shack. The four riflemen backed out and Fargo heard the lock close. Hallie's parting words lingered with him, in their own way a confirmation of the conviction that had been growing inside him. He went to the window and saw Hallie and Rupert Grandy going off together, their strides matching. They left his line of vision, and he let his eyes scan as much of the headquarters station as the window would permit him to see.

The station was a much busier place in the daylight. He watched men carrying lumber, others with a canoe that needed repairing, all Métis. He also saw a number of Métis women go by, some young and attractive, all carrying blankets of fruits and vegetables. He watched the passing scene into late afternoon, but neither Grandy nor Hallie appeared again. Finally, he turned from the window and began to examine the shack. He checked every corner and ran his hands over every inch of the walls. He hoped to find a loose board, a crack, a warped joint, anything he might widen or loosen with his knife, but there was nothing. The shack was too well constructed, and dusk was slipping through the window when he finished his inspection. He lay down on the cot, listening to the voices and sounds from outside die away as night fell. The muffled voices of the two guards from outside the door remained.

His lips thinned. He'd wait until the night was deep. Maybe they'd be half dozing by then, their hearing dulled. He'd go to work on the lock and hope they didn't hear him. If they did and came in after him he'd have to do the best he could. It was not a plan that made him optimistic, but he was down to his last option. He stayed on the cot and dozed, letting the night lengthen. When the time came he was awake and ready. As he prepared to sit up and follow through on his plan, a tiny shower of dirt and pebbles struck him. He swung to his feet and stared at the barred window as another handful of dirt flew into the room. He was at the window in two long strides, peering through the bars into the pale moonlight outside.

It took him a moment to make out the figure standing just below the window and astonishment swept through him as he saw the jet-black shock of hair first, then the handsome, high-cheekboned face beneath. "Monique," he breathed after he found his voice. She didn't hear his whispered word but she saw him and waved with one hand. Questions raced through his mind, tumbling wildly after one another and he cursed silently as he knew this was neither the time nor the place to ask even one. As his eyes stayed fixed on Monique another thought pushed its way through the barricade that kept in place all the questions he didn't dare try to ask. He thought of the other young attractive Métis girls he had seen walking past, and Monique would seem to be one more in their midst. The thought translated itself into whispered words.

"Can you hear me?" he asked and she nodded. "Two guards at the door. Flirt with them. Keep their attention." Monique nodded again and he saw her start to move to the corner of the house, her hips swaying boldly. He whirled, pulled the knife from the ankle holster and was at the door in a second. He paused and listened until he heard Monique's voice outside, then the guards responding. He heard her laugh flirtatiously. Dropping to his knees, he worked the knife into the lock. Monique's laughter grew louder, and he heard the guards joining in. She had their full attention. They weren't listening to him as he worked at the lock. Fargo swore as the mechanism resisted, but he worked the blade around the tumblers again, winced at the scraping sound from the lock.

The two guards were still busy with Monique when suddenly, he heard the lock snap open. He drew the knife out, stood up and slowly pushed the door open. Monique had drawn both men a few feet from the door, he saw. One had his arm around her waist while the other was holding her by the elbow. Fargo raised his hand, took aim and the throwing knife hurtled through the air. He had chosen the one holding her elbow. The other would take longer to disengage his grip on Monique and turn. In a half crouch, Fargo watched the blade strike with silent, deadly force, sinking itself to the hilt in its target. The man stiffened before crumbling to the ground.

The other turned at the sound and frowned as he stared down at the figure on the ground beside him. It took him a moment to collect his thoughts and start to pull away from Monique. But she caught hold of his wrist, costing him additional seconds to tear free of her grip. By the time he turned to bring his rifle up,

Fargo's blow caught him alongside the jaw. He went down on both knees and Fargo yanked the rifle from him, smashed the stock down on his head and the man pitched forward across his companion. "My horse is around back. Your Ovaro, too," Monique said. "I saw him tied beside the other shack and brought him along."

He kissed her. "You're a godsend. We'll talk after we get out of here," he said and followed her around to the rear of the house. "Walk your horse," he said as he led the Ovaro through the silence of the dark headquarters station. When they came to the main house he halted. "I'll be right back," he said and hurried into the big house and found his way to the wooden desk against one wall. His Colt lay on the desktop, Rupert Grandy's words echoing in his mind, and Fargo slid the weapon into his holster and returned to Monique. They continued to walk the horses, taking to the saddle only when they were beyond the last building by a hundred yards.

They rode until he found a deep cluster of cedar, turned into the trees and swung from the saddle. Monique was in his arms seconds after. "How did you get here?" he asked gratefully.

"I was going crazy just waiting and I heard rumours there might be another raid. I decided to go after you. I followed the river and reached the Split Lake station last night. I saw them take you into the guardhouse. She was there. What does that mean?" Monique said.

"You mean Heather?" he asked, and Monique nodded. "She wasn't Heather. She was Hallie," he said, and Monique's eyes widened as puzzlement crossed her face.

"What do you mean?" she asked.

He told her about the twin sisters and about everything else that had happened. Almost everything, leaving out the night with Hallie. "Heather is *delabré? . . . aliéné?*" Monique gasped. "*Mon dieu*. I told you there was something about her."

"You did," Fargo winced. "My mistake. I usually pay attention to female instinct. I'm a believer in it." An expression of fleeting triumph touched her face. "But there's something more going on here," he said.

"What?"

"Wish I knew," Fargo said. "But I don't believe they were afraid to take Heather back to the asylum. They preferred to concoct a clever scheme to kill her and use me to make sure it worked. Why?" Monique stared back, and finally shrugged. "That strange raid on the salmon shipment still doesn't sit right with me. When I asked Hallie about it she didn't seem bothered or much concerned. That didn't sit right with me, either. I want to go back there and have another look," Fargo said.

"They could have gone by now, unloaded their barrels at the schooners," Monique said.

"Maybe, but I want to see for myself," Fargo said.

"Alone? You'll be killed if they're still there. You almost were," Monique reminded him.

"Wasn't thinking of going alone," Fargo said, and Monique waited. "I was thinking of your people going with me," he said.

"What?" Monique frowned.

"You've a stake in these raids," he said. "All of you."

"How?" she questioned.

"Your jobs. If the raids put Grandy out of business

you'll be out of work. From what I've seen, the Métis around here are all working for Grandy."

"*Oui.*"

"It's time you stopped sitting back as if you weren't involved. Especially now when something strange is going on. I'm going to find out what. Talk to your people. Tell them to help me and themselves," Fargo said. "There must be somebody who's headman. Talk to him."

"Tomas Cetu. Everybody listens to Tomas. But I want you with me. It will help," Monique said.

"Where do we find this man? Time's important," Fargo said.

"He has a cabin in our village at Bear Lake."

"Let's go. You lead the way, but we move carefully. They've probably found out I'm gone by now. They'll have search parties out. We've one thing in our favor. They don't know about you. They'll be looking for the tracks of a single rider. Two horses together will throw them off some," Fargo said. Monique climbed onto her horse and rode close beside him as they left the cedars. He rode in as many stands of trees as he could find as Monique led the way south. They were in open land when he spotted three riders coming toward them.

"I've a gun," Monique said.

"No shooting if we can help it. Shots could bring others," Fargo said, reaching down to draw the knife from its ankle holster. He shoved it up into his sleeve, letting it rest where he could drop it into his palm instantly. He spoke to Monique without moving his lips. "You talk. Tell them I can't. I don't want them to hear me. They might have been told I'm an American," he said and halted as the three men rode up.

"Bonjour," Monique said.

One man with a hard, mustached, gruff face eyed her. "Métis?" he asked, his voice as rough as his face.

"Oui," Monique said.

The man brought his eyes to Fargo. "You?"

Monique answered. "He is my brother," she said.

"He can't talk for himself?" the gruff-voice said.

"He is *muet*—mute," Monique said.

The man's eyes stayed suspicious as they flicked to Monique and back to Fargo. "He doesn't look Métis," the man muttered.

Monique shrugged. "We are all different," she said. Fargo swore inwardly. It wasn't going well. The man was too suspicious. He didn't dare wait longer, he told himself. He had to use the slender advantage of surprise. But one of the others spoke up.

"It's not him. The one we're looking for is alone, nobody with him. Let's go," the man said.

"It is him," the gruff one snapped. "Look at the horse. How many Ovaros like that are around here?"

Fargo swore as he dropped the Arkansas toothpick into his hand, snapped his wrist and hurtled the blade, reaching its target in a fraction of a second. The gruff-faced man let out a gasp as he toppled from the horse. Fargo already had his Colt out and he lunged forward, lashing out and smashing the barrel across the forehead of the second rider. As the man fell forward in his saddle, Fargo brought the Colt down on his head. The man pitched from his horse but Fargo knew the third man had his gun drawn by then. Ducking low in the saddle, Fargo saw the man start to bring his gun up. Monique dove from her horse, and smashed into the man from behind. Taken by surprise, he fell sideways, Monique clinging to him. Both

110

hit the ground together as Fargo leaped from the Ovaro.

The man was still trying to escape from Monique's grasp when Fargo brought the Colt down on top of his head, and he went limp. Fargo reached down, pulled Monique to her feet and held her to him. "Saying thanks is getting to be a custom, one I like," he said as she clung to him and let her lips answer. "Let's get out of here," he said and gave her a hand onto her horse. In moments he was at a gallop beside her. Monique turned west as they raced across mostly open ground. They kept pace until Fargo saw the low-roofed buildings rise up before him, none more than a single story high, some square and some round, all forming a loose circle. A number of figures, both men and women, turned as Fargo rode up with Monique and dismounted just outside the largest of the circular structures. The house, made of wood, sod and canvas, echoed the medicine man lodges of some of the plains tribes, Fargo noted.

He also saw at least forty of the Métis Red River carts, their square wood and buffalo hide shapes and oversized two wheels pulled into a semicircle. Some were still hitched to oxen. The door of the circular house opened and a man stepped out, a short, slender, neat figure with a long face and a short, well-groomed beard. "Tomas," Monique said, stepping forward to warmly embrace him. Their conversation was animated, made of Indian, French and English of which Fargo could only catch an occasional word. When they finished, Monique brought the man to him. "Tomas Cetu," she introduced. "Tomas will help you."

"I'm grateful," Fargo said. "But people could be killed. I want you to know that."

"Monique explained that to me. But you are right. We cannot keep looking away. We are a part of all this whether we like it or not," Tomas said. "I have forty men to give you."

"That ought to do," Fargo said. He remembered there'd not been more than twenty or so with the canoes and dugouts. "We'll go downriver. When we near the spot, you take half the men and keep going. Sail right past them as if you were on your way someplace else. When you're out of sight you go ashore and work your way back on shore to them. I'll be ashore with the other half of your men below them. We'll have them between us when we attack."

"That is a good plan. But what if they have already left?"

"You'll know that when you pass the curve. If they've left you'll come back."

Tomas Cetu cast an eye at the horizon, where dusk had begun to settle. "I will gather the others, tell them what we must do and why. We will be ready in the morning," he said and turned to Monique. "There is freshly broiled *ouananiche* and wild rice in the cookhouse."

"Thank you, Tomas," she said, and her hand closed around Fargo's. She led him past a half-dozen small cabins to another circular structure, smaller and lower than the large one he'd seen. She took him inside and lit a candle as dusk became night. "I will be back," she said and slipped from the cabin. Fargo took in the deep piles of blankets on the floor and examined the wood, straw and canvas that formed the walls of the structure. There were plenty of little cracks and openings but he also noted a deep fire pit that would be more than enough to keep the small hut warm. He went outside, unsaddled the horses and was back in the round little structure when Monique appeared with the salmon and rice on a large, wooden palette, a bottle of wine tucked under one arm.

He sat down beside her on one of the blankets as they ate off of a small table with short legs. The meal was wonderfully satisfying, the wine a dark, rich sherry. "The schooners that come bring many things," she told him. He took the palette when they'd finished the meal. "Just put it outside. The night visitors will finish cleaning it up," she said and he carried the palette into the darkness, and placed it on the ground a dozen feet from the hut. When he returned, Monique lay on the blankets wearing only a sly smile. He paused to take in the beauty of her, his eyes lingering on her full-cupped breasts, moving down to the dense, black triangle and thighs that were so sensually curved. He shed his clothes as he moved to her and was half atop her in moments, as her hands pulled him over her. She pushed one pink-brown nipple against his lips and he opened, pulled it into his mouth and tasted the sweetness of its already firm tip.

"Ah, ah, yes . . . *oui, oui, cheri*," she murmured and let her hips grind against him, her convex little belly pushing against his, her body calling out in its own way. Her hands reached down, crawled along his hips, pushed over his groin, seeking, wanting, and her gasp of delight swept through the little hut as she found his waiting erectness. All the wild, simmering sensuality he had first seen in her returned and in moments the little hut seemed to shiver with the sound of her cries. She made love with every part of her body and her senses, totally immersing herself in the pleasures of Eros, and he was swept along into her wildness, reaching new heights of pleasure—with the sound of her cries, the sight of her black hair tossing from one side to the other and the touch of her body tingling against his.

When the moment came and she screamed, her head thrown back, her lips parted, and he felt her contractions pressing around him as he joined in the explosion of ecstacy, his own groans formed a deep obbligato to her cries. She finally collapsed against him, clinging with her arms, thighs and calves until her quivering finally died away. Her voice was a purring whisper when she spoke. "So good, so wonderful," she murmured. "It had to be this way."

"How do you mean that?"

"Special, because tomorrow may be a last day for us," she said.

"No, don't think that way," he said.

"Can you promise me it won't be?" she asked, and he swore softly. She smiled, a combination of wisdom and sadness.

"Then let us make it special again," she said, and he felt her lips find his, exchanging sweet beginnings and the little hut soon rang once again with her cries of ecstacy. He slept with her, finally, her soft body cushioned against him. Morning came in little slivers of light that crept into the round hut through tiny cracks and openings. Monique woke as he rose, wrapped herself in a blanket and led him out to a trough where they washed. He saw others gathering by the carts and picked out Tomas Cetu.

Returning to the hut with Monique, they dressed and she followed him outside where Fargo saw that eight of the Métis Red River carts had been set aside, still hitched to their oxen. "We leave our horses here," he said to Monique as they walked toward Tomas Cetu. A dozen women carrying cloth bundles were climbing into the carts along with men who carried rifles. "Why are they coming along?" he asked.

"There will be casualties. They bring bandages and sheets. Our doctor is at Atik Lake, north of here," she said. Tomas waved and he and Monique climbed into one of the carts alongside his.

"Ready?" he asked and Fargo nodded. Tomas barked out orders and the drivers snapped their whips, pushing the oxen forward. Fargo found that the two oversize wheels moved the carts with surprising smoothness. They reached the river in a little over a half hour and the men unhitched the oxen, then removed the long, slightly curved shafts. The wheels were left on as they pushed the carts into the river. In seconds, Fargo found himself gently bobbing on the water. Three of the men in the cart with him produced paddles and the carts began their journey downriver, wood and canvas rafts with sides. They moved slowly but finally neared the long curve in the river. Tomas, in the lead, slowed and waved at Fargo and went forward with half of the carts.

Fargo turned to Monique. "Tell the others to wait here till I get back," he said as he swung over the side of the cart and slid into the water. He struck out at once, powerful strokes that quickly brought him close to Tomas and the other carts. Swimming behind them, he watched as they began to round the curve. Keeping only the top of his head above water, he followed the carts around the curve and felt a moment of satisfaction. The canoes and dugouts were still there, as was the closed wagon, but the barrels were back in the boats. There were also another half-dozen canoes, he noted, which meant at least a dozen more guns.

The guards were still on shore, most of the others lounging in small groups nearby. Fargo treaded water as he saw them watch Tomas and the carts paddle past. But they didn't open fire, unwilling to draw attention to themselves. The carts were probably not the first crafts that had gone by along the river. As Tomas passed the spot, Fargo sank below the surface and swam back underwater until he was beyond the curve. He came up and swam back to where Monique and the others waited, waved them ashore and was on the bank to help put the carts onto dry ground. "Time to attack," he said and Monique reached into her skirt pocket and drew out a Lefaucheux six-shot, single-action French Navy revolver. He glanced at the others, who waited for his orders. "It'll be open land when we get near. We'll have to drop down and fire as we crawl or be sitting ducks," he said.

"The carts," Monique said. "They roll easily on those big wheels. We could push them."

His eyes went to the carts. "Rolling shields," he nodded. "Yes, by God. They'll give us some protection." He joined the others from his cart and began to push the square, wood and canvas cart forward and found that they did indeed move easily. He knew the rumble of the carts would be heard before they came into sight, but protection was worth trading for surprise. With the other carts spread out on both sides of him, he led the way around the curve and came into sight of the waiting cluster of men near the wagon and the canoes. It took another moment for the guards to recognize the approaching attack and to lay down their first volley of rifle fire. "Stay behind your carts," Fargo called to the others as he continued pushing forward. Finally he halted, dropped to one knee and fired back. One figure dropped from the knot of defenders and he saw two more go down as the Métis began to fire.

But the counterfire grew more accurate as the defenders spread out. Two bullets tore past where he and Monique crouched side by side when suddenly the volume of gunfire dramatically increased as Tomas's unit fired their first volley. The defenders raised, half turned to face this new and unexpected attack, surprised and off balance. Fargo fired a quick succession of shots and those near him did the same. At least six of the raiders went down and Fargo let himself spit out a grunt of satisfaction. Tomas's men were taking their toll, the two-pronged attack going exactly as he had hoped it would. Suddenly the air erupted with still another explosion of gunfire. Fargo whirled as a bullet tore through the top of the cart, hurtling in from his left. He saw three of the Métis go down as he stared across the narrow river to the other shore.

At least fifteen horsemen were racing along the shore, pouring bullets across the water. He saw the tall figure of Rupert Grandy, then found Hallie's auburn hair. "The Grandys. They've come to attack the raiders," Monique said. Three more bullets splintered wood from the cart as Fargo dropped flat and pulled Monique down with him.

"They're not firing at them. They're shooting at us," he bit out as four more of the Métis fell. Monique stared at him, her frown made of disbelief.

"The raiders have their salmon. They wouldn't be shooting at us," she said.

Six shots ripped through the canvas of the cart. "No?" he said. Monique stared at him, her face wreathed with incomprehension.

7

"Bullets now, talk later," Fargo said to Monique as he stayed flattened beside her. He fired across the narrow ribbon of water at Grandy's men and saw his shot miss. The riders were racing back and forth along the shoreline, pouring gunfire into the carts where he lay with the Métis, then racing down to do the same to Tomas and his crew. Fast moving, they would have been difficult targets even for expert riflemen. The Métis were having no success. Besides, the raiders, no longer caught in a cross fire, were laying down a deadly barrage of their own. Fargo cursed as he saw four of the Métis by the cart nearest to him go down. "We need better cover," he said and his eyes went to the line of red cedars a hundred yards behind them.

He turned to Monique. "Talk to them in your tongue. Tell them to leave the carts and run like hell for those cedars. Tell them to forget shooting, just run." She lifted her voice, called to those huddled beside the carts. When she finished, Fargo rose, pulled her up with them and streaked for the line of cedars in a zig-zag pattern. He glimpsed the others starting to follow as bullets slammed into the ground near him. Grandy's men adjusted their fire, but they were no longer shooting at stationary targets. Fargo reached the cedars untouched, and saw the others at his heels as he dove into the trees with Monique. He whirled, fired a shot off at the riders across the river and saw a figure topple from his horse.

Grandy's men fired back, but were no longer able to see their targets. Their shots went wild and Fargo saw Rupert Grandy wave his men back under a line of willows. They stopped firing as they disappeared under the long-branched trees. The raiders by their canoes also stopped firing, and an eerie silence descended over the scene. "Tomas and his men aren't shooting," Monique said. Fargo nodded and she read the grimness in his face.

"Oh, no. Oh, *mon Dieu*," she breathed. "You don't know. You can't be sure."

"No, I can't. But I suspect they'd be still shooting if there were any left to shoot," Fargo said and she turned away, her eyes closed for a long moment. Finally she pulled them open, peered across the river, then back to him. "I don't understand. They should be helping us, not the raiders who stole their salmon," she said. "I don't understand."

"I don't understand all of it, either, but it explains a lot," Fargo said, and her eye stayed on him, waiting. "It explains why Hallie didn't seem at all concerned when I told her about the raid. She never mentioned it again, never asked a question. Because she knew about it." Monique's frown deepened. "It explains why she and Grandy are here with their riders. They didn't just happen to be passing. They knew where the canoes and dugouts were. They came here to meet the raiders and found us here."

"To meet them?" Monique gasped.

"The Grandy's have been raiding their own salmon deliveries. They set it all up, made it all look like they were the victims when they were really behind all of it," Fargo said.

"Why? Why would they do that?" Monique asked.

"I don't know, but there's an answer, you can bet on that," he said.

"I . . . I cannot believe this—raiding their own company?" Monique said.

He broke off further talk as he saw three of Grandy's men come out from the willows and start into the river toward the cedars. Raising the Colt, Fargo let them get a half-dozen yards into the river before he fired. One of the riders flew backwards before he fell over his horse's rump and into the river. The other two leaped from their saddles and stayed beside their horses as they swam back to the shore and disappeared into the willows. "Why did they do that?" Monique asked.

"The army uses a french word, *reconnoitre*," he said.

"*Oui*, to explore, investigate," she nodded.

"Right. They wanted to see if we were here and what we'd do. They found out," Fargo grunted.

"What will they do now?" she queried.

Fargo glanced at the sky, saw the day sliding toward dusk. "They'll stay there and keep watch through the night in case we try to take to the river in the carts. Then they'll pick us off if we do," he said.

"The way you just did with them."

"That's right," he grunted.

"Which means they'll keep us trapped here," she said.

"Until they're ready to attack," he said.

"When will that be?" she asked.

"In the morning. They'll go downriver and cross, then come up on this side and join the others. They'll all come at us at once," he said.

"What if we wait till after dark, then try running out the other end of the cedars? We don't try to go by river," Monique suggested.

"By now they've sent someone back around to ride down to where the cedars end. There's a bright moon tonight. We'll be seen leaving the trees. One alarm shot and they'll catch us out in the open," Fargo said. "We won't have a chance."

"Then it is over. We are finished," Monique said glumly. He didn't answer as thoughts tumbled through his mind. Finally, he turned to her.

"Maybe not. There might be a way," he said. "They'll be watching the river. They'll see us if we all try to leave. They'll hear and see us if we try to use the carts. But two of us might be able to slide into the river without being seen. If we can get to your village at Bear Lake, we could bring back help."

"There are only a few women left at the village. Tomas brought everyone he could," Monique said.

"Damn," Fargo swore. "No guns and nobody to use them anyway."

One of the men nearby spoke up. "Maybe there is something. I am Paul Seenowa," he said.

"Paul is second to Tomas in our village," Monique said.

"There are six sticks of dynamite at our village," the man said. "We use dynamite to open waterways when beavers close them with their dams. It is the best and quickest way. Beaver dams are strong and hard to take down by hand."

"Six sticks," Fargo mused aloud. "It'll have to be enough."

"But it will take you near dawn to reach Beaver Lake by foot," Paul Seenowa said. "You won't get back in time for us."

"Don't plan to go on foot. There are enough rider-less horses out there that belonged to dead riders. I'll get hold of one of them."

"*Two* of them," Monique put in. He hesitated. "The women in the village don't know you. They won't help you. And I know where the dynamite is," she said and he nodded in agreement. Paul Seenowa left and Fargo sank down to the ground, leaning back against the grey-brown bark of a cedar. Monique sat beside him, her hand in his. "This is not your fight. But you stayed to help us. You are a good person, Skye Fargo," she said softly.

"You came to help me," he said. "Besides, they were going to kill me. That makes me angry and it makes it my fight." She leaned her head against him as night fell, letting herself doze, and didn't open her eyes until he gently shook her. "Time for a swim," he said. Paul Seenowa came over as Fargo rose to his feet. "I'll get back in time," he told the man with more confidence than he felt. Paul Seenowa nodded but Fargo thought he saw more gratitude than belief in his eyes. "Let's go," Fargo murmured to Monique. He stepped to the edge of the cedars and then flattened himself on the ground. He began to inch his way across the open land toward the riverbank with Monique beside him.

They reached the shoreline, and he swung himself around to edge into the water feet first. "Slow . . . slow," he whispered to Monique. "Don't make a ripple." She nodded and followed him as he eased himself silently into the water, submerging immediately and swimming underwater. He felt Monique swimming at his side and he stayed submerged until his lungs began to burn. He surfaced, treaded water, and saw Monique's head bob up nearby in the pale moonlight. They'd gone a dozen yards, he guessed. Not far enough. He took a deep breath and went under again. He swam another dozen or so yards before surfacing, waiting for Monique to rise beside him then peering back the way they had come. The hanging willows were in the distance and he struck out for the opposite shore. When he reached the bank, he lay motionless, Monique's body touching his.

He stayed still, his ears straining, taking in the sounds of the night creatures: flying, buzzing insects, the soft step of a raccoon pushing through brush near the water's edge. Suddenly he heard it—the sound of a horse blowing softly as it moved through the night. Another one sounded moments after. Both horses moved aimlessly, roaming the bank. Fargo rose to a crouch and started forward; Monique followed as he traced the sound. He wasn't concerned now about Grandy's men. They were far enough away in the willows, and their attention would be on the river. He saw the two horses come into sight, one behind the other and was about to straighten up and move toward them when two figures appeared.

"Shit," he swore under his breath as he remained on one knee and watched the two men move toward the horses. Grandy had sent out men to round up riderless mounts for his own uses.

"Easy, there," one of the men called to the two horses and Fargo cursed again.

"Stay here," he whispered to Monique as he moved from her and circled to the right to come up behind the two men as they moved closer to the horses. He knew he'd have to move fast enough to prevent their getting off even one shot. He crept forward on silent steps like a mountain lion on the prowl. The figure of the second man rose up in front of him, the first one almost at the horses. Neither of the horses moved as the men approached, steady mounts plainly used to several different riders. Fargo suddenly increased speed, coming up behind the second man as the first reached the nearest horse and started to climb up into the saddle. Fargo struck with silent power, his arm encircling the man's neck in front of him. A quick, twisting motion and the man's body went limp instantly. Fargo let him collapse to the ground, leaped over him and was at the second figure who had just settled into the saddle. Fargo reached out, grabbed the man's arm and yanked, seeing the surprise in the man's face as he was pulled from the saddle.

Hitting the ground, the man reached for his gun. He never got it out of its holster as Fargo's blow caught him flush on the jaw. He sprawled sideways and Fargo's Colt smashed down hard enough to end the short, vicious exchange. Straightening, Fargo saw Monique dashing toward him. "Your pick," he said, motioning to the horses. She chose the smaller animal, a short-legged but sturdy-looking roan. Fargo pulled himself onto the other horse. "Stay at a walk," he told her and held pace until they'd gone another few hundred yards, then he put the horses into a fast canter.

Monique was beside him as they rode out into open land.

This was her country, land she knew, so she led the way through shortcuts and passages that he might have missed in the night. He kept a steady pace behind Monique as the moon passed the midnight sky. When they reached Bear Lake, the village was dark and asleep, but he saw a half-dozen women emerge from their huts as he and Monique rode in. Monique went to the big, circular lodge while Fargo strode to where the Ovaro and Monique's horse were tethered under an overhang. He brought both back and met Monique emerging from the lodge. She carried the sticks of dynamite and a heavy cloth in which to wrap them. "I brought matches, too," she said. Fargo wrapped up the dynamite and placed the sticks in his saddlebag.

It was only minutes before they were riding back the way they had come. Time, in its malicious way, seemed to fly faster as they rode back, and Fargo cursed as he watched the moon's fast slide toward the horizon. But they both rode far better horses and the moon was still edging the horizon when they reached the river. Fargo rode hard along the shore until he crossed over to the far bank and kept his pace until the moon disappeared below the horizon. He slowed, but continued to ride forward until he reined to a halt and swung to the ground. "We walk from here," he said, and Monique followed behind him. The night had lost all light and the trees were dark, looming shapes of deep black. He used the river as his guide, and suddenly he saw the stand of cedars ahead of him.

The first rays of dawn were just tinting the sky

when he rode into the cedars and saw people rising to meet him. The figure of Paul Seenowa took shape as a ray of faint pink filtered through the trees. "You are indeed a special man," Paul said.

"Thank Monique. Don't think I could have made it without her help," Fargo said as he took the dynamite from his saddlebag. He gave two sticks to Paul, two to Monique and kept two for himself. "We'll use the dynamite. I want your men here in the trees to pick off those that get through," he said. "There'll be some," he added, reading the question in Paul Seenowa's eyes. "Dynamite is tricky. You plant it, set it to blow up logs and it'll work the way you want. You set it off in the open and it explodes in funny ways." The dawn began to lighten the interior of the treeline as Fargo stepped to the edge of the cedars, his gaze fastened on the figures clustered by the canoes. "They'll charge us when they're ready," he said. "Let them get within a hundred feet before you toss your dynamite, one stick at a time. Monique, you toss to the right, Paul, you to the left. I'll take the middle."

Fargo returned his gaze to where the knot of raiders stood in place. They hadn't moved and he was still watching them when Rupert Grandy arrived with his horsemen. He halted behind the raiders, settled in, but stayed in the saddle. Time passed and the new day's sun grew stronger but still, no one moved. Fargo felt the frown gathering on his brow and suddenly, a curse tearing from his lips, he whirled. "Everybody stay in place," he hissed as he started to run.

"What is it?" Paul Seenowa asked.

"Grandy's being real clever. He's going to try and

draw us off with a diversionary tactic, figuring we'll fall for it. Then he'll attack with his main force," Fargo said. "Stay in place, no matter what happens." He ran past the Ovaro, yanked the big Sharps from the saddlebag and kept running to the side edge where the line of trees ended. He dropped to one knee, his eyes slowly moving across the mixture of low brush and tall, scruffy weeds. He saw clusters of scraggly bushes that resembled brittle bush except in color. They were thick growths of four-foot butterweeds with a short, twisted under-brush. It took him a moment to spot the tips of the scraggly brush moving to his left, then another movement alongside it. His eyes counted six separate places where the brush moved. Six riflemen, he grunted, moving toward the cedars in a straight line.

He raised the big Sharps, letting the men come a little closer as he took aim just below where the first clump of brush quivered. He fired, swung the rifle and fired again, then kept swinging the gun and firing. Curses and cries of pain rose after each shot as the brush shook, the sound of bodies flailing following the screams. Fargo rolled, came up against a tree trunk and fired again, and a gargled cry of pain rose and ended just as abruptly. A short burst of return fire erupted, aimed at where he had been and his Sharps barked again. Fargo saw a clump of brush shake and a figure fall out through the stems and lie still. He saw the bushes violently quake as two men fled, crawling away as fast as they could. Fargo rose and hurried back to where the others were in place in the trees.

Shouts and the sound of pounding hooves greeted him as he reached Monique and Paul Seenowa. The horsemen were charging at the cedars from the front. They barreled straight on, plainly thinking that their diversion had pulled the defenders out of position. Lighting the fuse on the dynamite, Fargo tossed the stick high into the air, and watched it arc over the on-charging horsemen. It exploded in midair over their heads, and he saw three bodies catapulted to the ground. Monique and Paul had tossed their first sticks and Fargo saw them exploding to the right and to the left, and he glimpsed more bodies flying into the air.

Fargo tossed his last stick as did Monique and Paul. Screams of pain and curses mingled with the smoke. Through the haze Fargo spotted a half-dozen figures on foot still moving toward the cedars from the left and right edge. "Fire!" Paul Seenowa shouted and a volley of shots tore out of the trees. The six riflemen went down but three managed to get off shots and Fargo saw two of the Métis behind him fall. The women rushed to them both, bringing them towels and bandages. Fargo stepped to the edge of the trees in time to see Hallie, Rupert Grandy and four of his men racing away. They galloped past the canoes and dugouts before they turned and crossed the river to the other side, disappearing into the trees. Fargo stepped back and looked toward the women beside the two fallen Métis. "They are bandaging one. The other is gone," Paul Seenowa said.

"The Grandys have run," Monique said.

"We hit them hard. They'll need time to regroup," Fargo said. "Or they might try and sneak back by dark to take their merchandise. They may figure we'll leave it."

"Will we?" she asked.

Fargo grimaced. "I don't know," he said.

"I know we don't have any answers," Monique said as she walked from the trees into the open. He followed her as she neared the canoes and dugouts loaded with barrels. "Why did they arrange to have their own company raided? That's stealing from themselves. It doesn't make any sense," she thought aloud.

He glanced back at the bodies that littered the ground from the water's edge to the tree line. "I thought we might get some answers here, but dead men don't talk," he said. Striding to the closed wagon, he pulled the doors open. The wagon was empty inside except for a handful of small pieces of thin canvas that were meaningless to him. His eyes swept the scene, the boats, the river and the terrain. He returned to the wagon and he swore silently. Turning away, he felt Monique's eyes on him. "Dammit, I feel like I'm standing in front of something in plain sight but can't see it," Fargo said in angry frustration as he met Monique's eyes. "You're right, it doesn't make sense, but there has to be an answer. Somehow, it has to make sense. We just haven't found out how," he said.

"You said they weren't smuggling anything in place of the salmon. You looked at the barrels and there was nothing but salmon in them," she reminded him.

"That's right, dammit," Fargo snapped, then turned and started to walk away. He'd taken perhaps a dozen steps when he halted. He suddenly felt as if a burst of fire had exploded inside him, the thought growing, mushrooming, filling his entire being. He turned and stared at Monique. "That's right, I looked

130

in the barrels," he said. "But I didn't look in the salmon." He heard the surprise in his own voice and saw the frown gathering on Monique's brow as she stared at him. "The salmon, dammit," he bit out. "The salmon are gutted. Your people do it. They're big fish, with all the bones taken out. Damn."

He whirled and ran to the nearest dugout. Monique was beside him as he tore the lid from the barrel and pulled out one of the big salmon. Taking hold of one edge of the long slit cut into the fish's abdomen, he pulled it back and turned the salmon onto its side. An oblong, canvas-covered packet fell to the ground after a few shakes of the fish. Paul Seenowa came up as Fargo picked up the packet, unwrapped the canvas around it and stared down at the small, oblong-shaped yellow clump. "Gold," he breathed. "Gold flakes pressed into a brick. Son of a bitch," he swore and heard Monique's sharp intake of breath. But he was already pulling out another salmon, reaching into the barrel and pulling the fish's abdominal slit open. Another canvas-wrapped packet fell to the ground. Unwrapped, it held another oblong gold bar.

Monique and Paul pitched in, pulling salmon out of the barrel. When they finished opening the abdomen of each fish, they found that over half the salmon had held the bars of gold flakes. "This is your answer," Fargo said. "They're using the salmon to smuggle gold past the inspectors on the schooners. The raiders hijack the salmon, fill them with the gold bars and take them to the schooners. When the inspectors open the lids on the barrels, they see only tightly stacked salmon, just as I did. I can put the rest together. Somebody at one of the ports, probably in the States, is waiting and buys the whole shipment."

"But that doesn't explain it all," Monique said. "The Grandy's have the salmon. They could put the gold bars inside themselves. Why did they arrange this charade that had everyone believing raiders were stealing the salmon?"

"Exactly for that reason. They were being real clever. If an inspector found the gold, they'd be in the clear. Everyone knew their shipments were being raided. The raiders who brought the salmon would be blamed, arrested and hung, nobody else," Fargo told her. "The only reason they showed up here is because they knew I would. Hallie had found out I knew too much. They didn't want to take any chances so they came here to get me. They didn't know I'd have all of you with me."

"The gold has to come from somewhere in Saskatchewan," Paul Seenowa put in. "I have heard stories that gold shipments were caught going across the border into America. I guess they decided this was a safer way to ship it. Of course, it is anyone's guess who is waiting to buy it in your country."

"I can make one guess," Fargo said. "There's talk about a war between the States. I heard the south is amassing gold in case that happens."

"What do we do, now?" Monique asked. "We are not gold smugglers or raiders. We would only be caught."

"Let your wounded go back to Bear Lake. The rest of you take the canoes and dugouts. Go to the schooners where they're waiting. Show the inspectors what you have. Tell them you came onto it by chance.

132

I'm sure there'll be a sizeable reward, usually a percentage of the value of the gold," Fargo said.

"That will be more money than we have ever had," Paul Seenowa said.

"Especially added to the half-dozen bars you'll forget to include," Fargo said, keeping his face expressionless.

"Yes, that could happen," Monique said after a moment. Her hand found his. "You will come with us," she said.

"Can't," he said, and she frowned. "Got some unfinished business. Heather and Hallie. I'm going to take them both in."

"No," she said, her face growing tight. "You can't go after them."

"Both of them should be under lock and key, one because she needs it, the other because she deserves it."

"What about Rupert Grandy?"

"I'll take him in, too," Fargo said.

"I'll go with you," she said.

"No. Go back to Bear Lake with the others. This is for me to finish," he said.

"I helped you last time," she said.

"Yes, and you've done more than enough. I'm not going to let you risk your life again," he said.

"You're risking yours," she countered.

"I've made a lifetime of that. Besides, Hallie will come looking for me. So will Rupert Grandy. Heather will, too, if she can. It'd be just like Hallie and Grandy to give her that chance. It'd work to their advantage. I have to stop that before it starts," he said. He pulled her to him and found her lips with his. "It's best this way. Believe me."

"I will be at Bear Lake. Don't make me wait forever," she said, walking away from him without looking back. Fargo turned, found the Ovaro and crossed the river.

8

It was past mid afternoon when he reached Split Lake and the Grandy headquarters. The first thing he noted was the silence—there was not a sound to be heard, not a figure to be seen. Dismounting, Fargo left the pinto and carefully walked forward, his eyes sweeping the nearest buildings. The one in which they were holding Heather was marked in his mind. It was the one behind the large, main building. Grandy had taken four men with him when he fled the river. They were here, waiting. Fargo saw a water trough just outside the nearest building. He crossed to it in a crouch and dropped down beside it.

Flattening himself on the ground, he let his ears become his eyes, letting each sound become a message. Grandy was smart. He had proven that. He wouldn't suddenly become stupid. Fargo put himself in the man's shoes, tried to think as he did. Grandy was smart enough to know he had his limits. He had four ordinary men left and he'd have to use them in ordinary ways. He had no choice. They weren't capable of anything more. Grandy wouldn't expect them to rise above their natural limits. He would simply hope that they got lucky.

He'd position one as the front man, almost a kind

of sacrificial goat. Fargo grunted. He had a lot more than luck to rely on, he knew, and he stayed motionless as his ears strained for the slightest sound. The men had to have heard him when he rode up and were probably already positioned. But they were neither hunters, trappers nor trailsmen. They were hired gunslingers and gunslingers were always short on patience. Fargo only had to wait. As it turned out, the wait was shorter than he'd expected. The sound of a pebble being dislodged reached his ears. He pinpointed it instantly. It was close by, at the corner of the building. He inched forward again, the Colt in his hand, his finger resting on the trigger.

He spotted the man as he appeared, a six-gun in his hand. The man's gaze swept the scene, and he suddenly saw the figure alongside the trough. Startled, he started to bring his gun up but the Colt barked first. The figure shuddered and staggered back. His shirt was stained red as he fell. Fargo's eyes were already on the roof of the next building and he saw the head appear over the edge of the roofline. Fargo raised the Colt but the head pulled back instantly. Fargo leaped to his feet and raced to the building, slamming into the door with his shoulder. The door flew open and Fargo dove inside, hit the floor and rolled. He came up against a table and stayed in place. His eyes instantly found the narrow stairway that led to a doorway to the roof.

His glance traveled around the rest of the room, seeing it was a storage place with everything from rakes and shovels to miscellaneous pieces of board and lumber. His eyes returned to the door at the top of the stairs. The man was on the roof, waiting for him to come up, ready to pour lead into him the minute he set foot through the door. Again, Fargo's glance took in the room as he pushed to his feet. A long piece of wood beckoned to him. He estimated it to be six feet in length. He uttered a grunt of satisfaction as he took the long polelike length of wood and began to silently climb the narrow stairs. He'd do exactly what the man on the roof expected him to do. Almost.

When he reached the top of the stairs, he put the Colt down on the top step, then lay down flat on the stairs. Taking a firm grasp of the pole with both hands, he paused, listened for a moment and smiled. He could see the man in his mind, a few feet back of the door, gun in hand, ready to blast a volley of shots. Gathering every muscle in his arms, shoulders and back, Fargo raised the pole and, still lying flat on the top steps, drove the length of wood into the door. Instantly, the door flew open revealing the man waiting not more than three feet back. The man fired, emptying his six-gun in an automatic reaction, pouring lead through the doorway. But his target lay flat, the shots pouring over his head.

The minute the door flew open Fargo's hand curled around the Colt that had been lying at fingertip's reach. He fired two shots as a hail of bullets whistled over his head. The man staggered backwards, his mouth falling open, his gun hand going limp. He continued to stagger back, the edge of the roof only a few feet behind him. He hit it as he started to collapse. Fargo watched his figure topple over the edge. Fargo lifted himself up and backed down the stairs. The man had landed with a thud, the shots had shattered the air. No doubt the last two of Grandy's men had heard. Would they have the self-discipline to stay low and wait? Or would they give way to their normal, undisciplined selves, giving in to fear and uncertainty? Fargo bet on the latter. To gunslingers, discipline was measured in seconds.

He reached the ground floor of the building and saw a pile of small squares of wood. He gathered eight pieces and put them into his pockets. Stepping outside, he edged his way along the side of the building to where he had a view of the buildings beyond. The main office building was the largest, rising up a dozen yards from him. Two doors fronted the structure, four windows on each side. It was the kind of place they'd choose, giving them plenty of room to hide and maneuver inside. Fargo slid down at the edge of the building and leaned against the wall, allowing him to see the front of the main building. He relaxed and let time go by, letting minutes slide into hours. He'd seen nothing move along the ground, behind the main structure or at either side. He grew increasingly certain that they were holed up inside, their nerves frayed to the edges by now. He decided he'd try for a little more proof just to be sure.

Dusk was starting to slip over the land when Fargo finally edged his way forward. He took one of the blocks of wood from his pocket and threw it. It sailed through the air and hurtled into one of the windows with a loud crash. A shot followed instantly and Fargo smiled. He settled back and let dusk turn into night. As soon as night wrapped the buildings in front of him in blackness, he rose, crossed the open ground to the main building and slowly turned the doorknob, pausing every split second to keep the lock from clicking. Finally he felt the door give, and he eased it open, paused, crouched and then slid his way into the building. He closed the door just as carefully, letting the lock turn a fraction of an inch at a time until it closed.

He stayed motionless, his ears straining as the moon filtered in through the windows. It allowed no more than a pale glow, outlining some of the clutter he remembered from the large room: skis, snowshoes, a cabinet, boxes, crates, the long table. But he was not alone in the big room. The shot had proven that. The only question was whether he had the company of two gunslingers or one. His company was hunkered down amid the assortment of objects, waiting and growing more nervous and tense with each passing second. Moving ever so carefully, he drew another of the blocks of wood from his pocket, raised his left arm and tossed it into the corner across from him. It landed with a sharp, bouncing sound, not unlike someone stumbling. Two shots erupted at once. One came from almost directly in front of him, the other from across the far side of the room.

Fargo drew another block of wood from his pocket. He kept his eye on the clutter of snowshoes and boxes across from him as he tossed the block. He threw it so it would land only a few feet from the first and seem as if someone had stumbled again. It struck the ground and skittered to one side, and Fargo saw the dark outline of a figure rise, the flash of his two shots cutting through the darkness. Fargo fired, aiming just behind and below the flash of gunfire. He saw the figure half spin and heard the guttural sound tear from the man's lips as he pitched forward. He knocked aside four snowshoes as he fell sprawling to the floor where he would eventually lie still.

Remaining motionless, Fargo's gaze focused on the far corner. He had expected the second gunslinger to fire also, but the man had held back. Fargo cursed as he flung himself sideways in a rolling dive, and he heard the shots slam into the doorway where he had just been. He kept rolling as the man followed the sound of his movement, the bullets slamming into the floor only inches away from him. Fargo came up against a wooden crate and pushed himself behind it. The man fired two more shots that tore into the top of the crate. Fargo hardly breathed as he stayed motionless, listening. He heard the unmistakable click of a cylinder being swung open—the other man was reloading. Fargo half rose and fired, spraying shots at the location the man had fired from.

He heard the man curse, then the sound of his gun hitting the floor as he lost his grip on it while falling back to avoid the bullets bracketing him. Fargo tried to fire again and heard the hammer fall on an empty chamber. "Shit," he swore and heard the man moving, saw his dark bulk racing across the room for the door. Fargo holstered the Colt as he leaped up and streaked across the room, his angle letting him reach the door just as the other figure did. He dove, tackling the figure and they both went down. Fargo felt a knee sink into his groin and as he fell away, he saw the man rising. The large, bulky man lashed out with a roundhouse left that Fargo could only partly block. His opponent was clearly powerful as the blow sent Fargo sailing backwards. With a roar of rage the bulky figure rushed at him, but this time Fargo had the split second he needed to set himself and get off a hard, straight left. It landed on the man's jaw and the man wavered, reeling a step backwards.

Fargo followed with a crashing right and the man went down. Stepping forward, Fargo tried to bring another blow crashing down but the man rolled, and regained his feet. As he surged forward, Fargo could only make out a wide, flat face in the half-light. He aimed a blow at it, feinted and the man reacted, ducking to his right just as Fargo's left caught him high on the cheekbone. He staggered back a few steps and tried to weave but Fargo's following right came in hard. The man crashed into a dozen skis stacked against the wall. Fargo loosed a tremendous left hook that snapped the man's head around and saw the figure go down face forward into the skis that had crashed to the floor. Moving forward, Fargo slowed and heard a half strangled sound from the figure on the floor. The man's legs jerked spasmodically, his entire figure quivered for a moment and then suddenly he lay still. Moving carefully, Fargo stepped to him, turned him over and saw that the man's throat was punctured. The sharp tip of one of the skis was covered with blood from where he had fallen onto it.

Fargo let a long sigh escape him as he turned away and went outside. He reloaded the Colt as he did, his actions smooth and steady, almost like a reflex. He leaned against the outside wall of the building when suddenly he heard the sound of a horse galloping into the darkness. The sound came from the rear of the complex of buildings. Rupert Grandy was fleeing. He had waited, listened, undoubtedly counted each shot he heard, and waited to hear some sign of victory from his four gunslingers. But none had come. He knew it was time to hightail it out of there.

Fargo knew it would be hard to follow his tracks in the night, besides, he had other things to finish. He turned and strode to the cabin where Heather had been held prisoner. He saw the flickering light of a candle through the lone window, reached it and paused, one hand on the door. He wondered if Heather was alone inside, or if Hallie was with her. "Come in," a voice called. His hand on the Colt in its holster, he opened the door and stepped in having no idea whose voice he had heard. Two tall, slender figures were facing each other, one holding a British Westley Richards six-shot, single-action revolver, the other a Remington-Beals five-shot piece.

Were it not for the bruise still visible on Heather's cheek he would not have been able to tell them apart. They faced each other, guns pointed, but both turned their heads as he entered. Hallie spoke first. "Don't do anything stupid or I'll kill you, first," she said. "None of this would have happened if you hadn't helped her."

He looked at Heather. "I'll kill you, too," she said with an offhand shrug.

"I helped you, too," he said.

"Not enough," she spat.

His eyes flicked to the gun in Heather's hand. "How'd you come by that?" he asked.

Hallie answered. "She stole it from one of Daddy's men when he brought her some water, took it from him without him knowing about it."

"He was stupid and I enjoyed it," Heather said. Fargo's thoughts raced. He'd try to keep them talking until he could reach one of them. Hallie offered the best chance. She was thoroughly evil, but she still clung to reality. Her question proved that.

"Why are you still here?" she queried.

"Came to take Heather back. It's the right thing, the right place for her," he said.

"And me?" Hallie said.

"Got the right place for you, too," he said. "Unless we can work out something better."

"You won't. You're not the kind," Hallie sniffed disdainfully.

He looked at Heather, then Hallie. "How long have you two been facing off here?" he asked.

"Almost an hour, since I came to get her," Hallie said.

"And found I had the gun," Heather continued with a little laugh. "She insists on standing in my way."

"What way?" Fargo frowned.

"It's Daddy I want. He let them put me into the asylum. He's going to pay for that," she snapped.

"There's been enough payback," Fargo said soothingly. "I came to help you, Heather."

"Don't want your help, not anymore, don't want it and don't need it," Heather said. Fargo cursed inwardly and his eyes went to Hallie.

"I can help you, too," he said. "Let's try to work something out," he tried.

Hallie uttered a derisive grunt. "Heather doesn't want you and I don't believe you," she said.

"Let's shoot him together," Heather cut in, a burst of enthusiasm in her voice. "That'll sure be different."

Fargo saw Hallie consider it for a moment. "Why not?" she said, and Fargo swore silently. They were too close. They couldn't miss and he'd never get a shot off in time. As he watched, both turned their guns from each other, pointing their barrels at him. He felt his lips pull back in helpless despair as he saw Hallie start to tighten her finger on the trigger. But as she did, Heather's gun swung back to her and the Remington fired. Hallie's body buckled and she took

143

one step sideways. She turned to stare at Heather, her mouth agape, disbelief flooding her face as her chest began to bloom red.

Fargo flung himself forward in a diving tackle. Heather hadn't acted to save him. He knew she wasn't capable of such a grand gesture. Proof he was right came as she turned the gun back and fired. But he was already diving and her shots went whizzing over his back. He slammed into her at the knees, and she went down, firing off another shot. He got one hand on her wrist and twisted, and the gun fell from her hand. She lifted a knee and drove it into his groin, knocking him back. He got his arms up in time to avoid her clawing nails as she flew at him. Rolling backwards, he got to his feet as she tried to reach for the gun. He got to her first and flung her halfway across the room. She landed hard, groaned and slumped half conscious.

He turned and knelt down beside Hallie. The disbelief still flooded her face, her eyes staring emptily up at him. He returned to Heather, lifted her to her feet as consciousness came back to her. He pushed her from the little hut, gripping her firmly with one hand twisted behind her back. He marched her to where the Ovaro waited, took a length of lariat and tied her hands in front of her so she could hold on to the saddle horn. He found a horse nearby and lifted her onto it.

"You won't take me back," she said almost airily.

"Whatever you say," he answered, aware that the time for words had gone by forever. She lived in her own world with its own dragons and demons. Hallie had lived in hers, with another set of demons. Twins, he murmured, two sides of the same fatal coin. He led

144

the way out of the area but did not go too far before he found a stand of juniper and bedded down. He kept Heather securely tied hand and foot to a tree. When morning came, he untied her so that she could wash at a stream. She undressed and washed slowly, laughing at him the entire time as he took in her beauty.

"Still want to take me back?" she asked as she toweled herself dry, making certain he saw every lovely curve of her breasts, the beauty of her full-fleshed body.

"Never said I wanted to," he answered, tying her hands again when she was dressed.

"You won't," she said with an almost placid confidence. He turned partway back to the Grandy headquarters, his eyes searching the ground until he found the hoofprints he wanted—a single horse racing from the rear of the buildings. He turned and followed the prints, Heather at his side watching him scan the ground.

"Who are you following?" she asked.

"I'm not sure," he lied, and she fell silent. The hoofprints led north, and he saw where the horse had slowed, then where the rider had camped. He went on for another half mile when the tracks suddenly disappeared at the edge of a rock plate that stretched on with a stand of quaking aspen alongside one edge. Grandy had taken to the rock to avoid leaving a longer trail. But the rock was hard on a horse, slippery and treacherous. He'd not stay on it, Fargo decided and turned the Ovaro into the aspen. He stayed in the trees and soon found the hoofprints again. Grandy was walking his horse, the prints told him. Fargo put the Ovaro into a trot, bringing Heather along with him. He went another thousand yards when he slowed, halted and dismounted. Grandy's horse had developed a limp.

"Get off," Fargo told Heather and helped her slide from the horse. He tied her securely to a strong branch.

"You're not going to leave me here, are you?" she said, fear tingeing her words.

"Not for long," he said and hurried away. He followed the prints on foot for perhaps another few thousand yards, then he slowed and moved forward cautiously. The aroma of coffee reached his nostrils. Poking through the trees, he saw Rupert Grandy squatting down before a tiny fire, heating a coffeepot. His horse stood against a tree nearby. Fargo stepped forward. "You can finish that at the province jailhouse," he said.

Grandy spun and rose, letting the coffeepot drop onto the fire. A look of surprise sprung across the man's face. "You're a tenacious man, Fargo," he said.

"And you're a coward, Grandy, deserting both your daughters after your last four boys failed you," Fargo said. "But you're the kind of coward who'll come back to try and pick up the pieces. But not this time." His eyes cut to the horse, and he saw the swelling at its fetlock. The animal was unrideable until the swelling had a chance to go down. "Drop your gun and kick it over here," he told Grandy. "Nice and slow." The man shrugged and did as he'd been told. Fargo picked up the gun as it skidded to a halt at his feet. "Start walking," Fargo commanded.

"Got some shirts, personal things in my saddlebag," Grandy said. "Also got a nice bit of money stashed away. It's yours if you want it."

"Get the things from the saddlebag," Fargo said, and Grandy shrugged as he walked to the horse. He was reaching into the saddlebag when Fargo saw him spin. His hand came out of the bag with the six-gun in it. Fargo dropped as Grandy fired, the bullet plowing into the tree behind him. Fargo drew the Colt as he rolled and felt another bullet crease him, tearing through his shirt. Still another hit the tree trunk as he reached it. He whirled, staying low, and saw Grandy streaking to reach a tree. The Colt fired a single shot, and Rupert Grandy smashed into the tree, slowly sliding down to the base, his arms around it as if clinging to it protectively.

Fargo grimaced, walked to the horse and took the saddle from it, then the bit and reins. He knew the animal would find its own way. Rupert Grandy had found his and it had been the wrong way. Walking slowly, Fargo reached the Ovaro and rode the rest of the way to where Heather waited. "Looks like you struck out," she said.

"In a way," he said as he untied her from the tree and returned her to the horse.

"Where now?" she asked.

"Bear Lake," he said.

"And then?"

"Manitoba," he muttered.

Heather gave him a wide, charming, lovely smile. "You won't take me back," she said. "I just know it." He didn't answer. She had enclosed herself in her world. They rode on and she didn't speak for another hour. "I know a shortcut to Bear Lake," she said.

"I'm listening," he said.

"We have to go over a high rock promontory, some ice always clinging to it. It's a very narrow road but any good horse can go it. It'll cut hours off the time to Bear Lake," she said.

"Let's go," he said and went with her as she showed the way north, then west. The ground rose and finally he saw the high, granite slopes with ice at the tops of what would be a forbidding climb. A narrow road circled the high rock with a sheer drop at one side.

"It looks worse than it is," Heather said. "I used to ride it all the time." He nodded and they went forward, reaching the narrow road as it rose up, circling the side of the granite slabs, then dropping at the other side some few hundred feet onto more rock.

"I'll be right behind you," he said and let her go first. The curving path was plenty wide enough for two horses side by side, but he decided to stay behind Heather. Keeping at a slow walk, she led the way up the curving pathway that hugged the granite slopes on one side. Finally, when they reached the top, she began the descent. She turned and smiled back at him.

"I told you it wouldn't be so bad," she said.

"You were right," he nodded.

"Just like I told you you won't take me back," she smiled again.

"I have to. It's the best thing for you," he said.

Her smile grew wider but he thought he caught a hint of disappointment in it. She turned her attention back to riding, and he stayed a length behind her when suddenly she rose in the stirrups. He felt his mouth fall open, his eyes widen as he saw her jump, using the stirrups as leverage. She twisted her body, clearing the horse, and he heard his own shouts of protest as she dove down the side. Her body twisted as she plunged down the sheer drop. He yanked the Ovaro to a halt, leaped from the saddle and dropped to one knee at the edge of the path. She was just a tiny form now, hurtling end over end to the bottom of the rocks.

He looked away, then slowly pushed to his feet, feeling the heaviness inside him. He stood beside the Ovaro for a long time before he pulled himself into the saddle. His lips moved silently. *You won't take me back. I know it,* she had said. He had heard her, heard the words, but not understood their real meaning. But then, Heather's world was a place of its own, private meanings.

9

The village at Bear Lake had settled itself, the wounded were treated and the dead were buried. Monique clung to his arm as she and Paul Seenowa listened while he told them everything that had happened. When he finished, it was Paul Seenowa who spoke first.

"Among our people, there is a saying. 'The mad see in ways we cannot see, do in ways we cannot do and understand in ways we cannot know,'" he said.

"Sometimes things end the way they are meant to end, and you can't change that," Monique added.

"The Grandy Trading Company is no more," Fargo said, "but there is a market and a demand. People want the *ouananiche*. You can deal with the trappers, the Indians, the *couriers de bois*. Monique knows how it is done. Your people have done the work for others. Now you can do it for yourselves. You can be the Métis Trading Company."

Paul stared back for a long moment, exchanging glances with Monique. Fargo saw the excitement forming in his eyes as the thoughts inside him quickly mushroomed and took hold. "Yes, yes," he breathed. "Why not?"

"We could do it," Monique said, her own excitement catching hold in her voice.

"We will do it!" Paul almost shouted.

"Then something good will have come from all this," Fargo said.

Monique linked her arm in his. "After I finish showing you Manitoba," she said.

"Now, that's a great idea," he said.

"I'll get my things," she said and hurried away. He was waiting on the pinto when she returned, extra bags tied to her horse. "We will go west. There are many nice places there," she said.

"And you, the nicest of them all," he said.

It was later that night, after he'd found a place to camp in a jack pine forest, that she made the night simmer into ecstacy. As she lay against him, satisfied and warm beside him, she let her thoughts idle. "I keep thinking of all that happened," she murmured. "Twins. I can still hardly believe it. How did you know? You must have seen them together."

"No," he said and bit his tongue as her next question stabbed into him.

"Then how did you find out? What made you know?" she asked.

He thought for a moment. "They laughed differently," he said. It wasn't a lie, he told himself. Not exactly. Laughter . . . orgasms, they were both part of the same thing—enjoying life.

"Nobody else would have noticed that," she said. He allowed a modest shrug as he breathed a sigh of relief. He didn't want to make a habit of having all his sight-seeing trips ruined.

LOOKING FORWARD!
The following is the opening
section from the next novel in the exciting
Trailsman **series from Signet:**

THE TRAILSMAN #230
FLATWATER FIREBRAND

1860—the broad plains of Nebraska, where unwary
travelers fall prey to the lowest of vermin, and where
justice is painted in broad strokes of crimson red and
gunmetal blue....

Pooter McCoy was drinking straight from the bottle
now, and it wasn't making him any nicer.

Skye Fargo peered over the rim of his whiskey
glass as he downed the last of the rotgut, his gaze
fixed on the skinny little weasel who was dealing stud
at a table a dozen or so yards away. They were in a saloon called the Buffalo Chip, in the town of Flatwater,
Nebraska Territory.

Pooter McCoy stood about five feet six inches and
weighed less than a damp ironing board. His hair was
like straw, his chest sunken, his forehead high, and
Fargo figured he could count McCoy's teeth on the
fingers of one hand. His eyes were closer together
than any eyes had a right to be. Pooter McCoy was
doubtless the product of kissin' cousins.

The town of Salinas, Kansas, wanted McCoy for
slaughtering two innocent souls in a poorly planned

bank robbery, in which McCoy's brother, Bug, was also killed. Pooter drilled the clerk with lead and, in the confusion, a parson's wife who just happened to scream at the wrong moment.

Pooter McCoy escaped without a penny, but escape he did. There was blood on his hands and a price on his head, a very tidy thousand dollars. With some careful arithmetic, Fargo reasoned, he could live fairly comfortably for several months on a thousand. But if women and whiskey were involved, and they usually were, the reward would last a few weeks.

Fargo had picked up McCoy's trail a little south of Omaha and tracked him all the way here. Fargo's journey was ten days old, and he was ready to end it, then sleep until his next birthday. He placed his shot glass back on the bar.

The bartender, a tubby sort of a fellow, asked, "Again?"

Fargo nodded. Filling the glass, the bartender commented, "Smells like snow."

Fargo said, "This town smells like a lot of things, but snow ain't one of them." The bartender grunted something, scooped some wet coins off the bar, and went away.

Fargo watched as McCoy started dealing the next hand—from the bottom, not surprisingly—taking a long swig from the bottle after the last card was dealt. With him at the table were a couple of local cowboys and a citified dandy in a dusty suit and derby hat. A drummer most likely, from back East. The locals didn't seem to notice McCoy's sloppy cheating methods, probably because they were as sloshed as he was. The drummer, though, looked frightened. Like Fargo, he had doubtless seen his share of inbred, neck-bowed hard cases like Pooter McCoy, men with a low tolerance for whiskey and a high one for violence.

The drummer wisely threw in his cards after the hand was dealt and said, "Too rich for my blood." He hastily grabbed his money from the table and made his way to the bar, where he ordered a whiskey.

The drummer said to Fargo, "Man would be a fool to stay in that game."

Fargo said nothing, watching McCoy win another hand. He took another healthy slug from the bottle and let out a belch that echoed into the next territory. It was just a matter of time before the dumbhead cowboys got wise to McCoy's half-assed card tricks, and then all hell would break loose. Fargo hoped to avoid this.

The drummer said, "If you were thinking about getting into that game, mister, I'd strongly advise against it. Not only is that boy a piss-poor cheater, my innards tell me he's prone to violence."

"You reckon?" Fargo asked.

"In my line of work," the drummer said, motioning for a refill, "I can smell trouble a mile away. Pure Arkansas trash, that one."

"He's from Missouri," Fargo said.

The drummer went on, "Crimp's the name, Hiram Crimp. Armstrong Anvil Company, Pittsburgh, Pennsylvania. And a better judge of character you'll not meet."

Fargo watched as McCoy sucked down the last of the backwash in the bottle and hollered for another.

The bartender seemed reluctant to bring it, knowing that little good would come from Pooter McCoy having more to drink.

Fargo saved him the trouble. He slapped a silver dollar on the bar and said to the bartender, "Let me buy the lad a drink."

The bartender looked uncertain until McCoy flung the empty whiskey bottle across the saloon, where it missed the piano player by a good inch and a half, shattering against the wall. "Bring me another bottle, dammit, or I'll blow yer head off!" McCoy shouted.

What happened next would become the stuff of legend in Nebraska Territory for decades to come and make the Buffalo Chip Saloon a landmark.

Fargo took the full whiskey bottle from the bartender and uncorked it, never taking his eyes off Pooter McCoy. The bartender said to Fargo, "I hope you know what you're doing, friend."

"So do I," Fargo replied, grabbing a couple of glasses off the bar.

"Sir, as I said—" Hiram Crimp began.

"I know," Fargo said, walking slowly toward McCoy and the cowboys. "A better judge of character I'll never find."

As he walked, Fargo planned his next move. McCoy wouldn't be taken alive, of that Fargo was sure, but he had to at least try. And the cowboys at the poker table would have to go, and quickly.

Clutching the whiskey bottle and the glasses, Fargo sat down at the table and said, "Mind if I join in?"

Even drunk, Pooter McCoy's lifeless black orbs burned with suspicion. Before he could answer, Fargo

poured him a drink, then one for himself. The cowboys, who couldn't have been older than eighteen,
pushed their empty whiskey glasses toward Fargo,
licking their lips.

"You boys are too young to drink," Fargo said to
them.

One of them opened his mouth in angry protest.
Fargo shot him a stare that shut him up quick. The
boys took the hint, scooping up their money and bid-
ding their farewells.

"Looks like it's just you and me," Fargo said. He
raised his glass to McCoy and added, "To your health,
Mr. McCoy."

McCoy was quick. Crying out in a ferocious animal
yowl, he dropped the whiskey glass, which was
halfway to his bloodless lips, and kicked back from
the table, starting to rise and go for the holster on his
right hip.

Fargo upended the table right into McCoy, sending
cards, glasses, and poker chips flying. Fargo was on
his feet and reaching for the Colt and, in that next
split second, was horrified to see that McCoy was up,
and had somehow sidestepped the poker table. He
was also clearing leather. He fired once at Fargo, who
was already diving to his left, out of the way. The bullet whizzed by him; Fargo heard a distinctively wet
splat. McCoy cried out again, a bloodcurdling shriek
of hate and anger. In the years to come, bartender Eustace McGonigle would describe it to customers as
"the most god-awful, inhuman sound these ears have
ever heard, or will ever hear."

Fargo hit the floor, rolled once, and was up. The

Colt was rock steady in his hand. He fired, and the bullet cut a wide, deep-crimson swath against the side of McCoy's head, taking the best part of his right ear with it. McCoy cried out in pain and fired back wildly, the blood in his eyes momentarily blinding him. Fargo dodged again, but was up before McCoy could blink a third time. Fargo aimed and squeezed off another shot, and this time hit pay dirt. The bullet smashed into McCoy's cheek half an inch below the eye and blew out the back of his head.

McCoy dropped like a sack of brass doorknobs. For a moment there was absolute silence, then the piano player moaned and fainted dead away, collapsing off his stool into a heap on the sawdust-covered floor.

"Shit on fire and save the matches," Eustace McGonigle muttered in a small voice.

Fargo made his way over to McCoy's lifeless carcass and prodded him with his boot. It never hurt to be sure. He looked down at the gaping hole in McCoy's head, thick black blood oozing like molasses. Pooter McCoy wouldn't be shooting another pastor's wife anytime soon.

"I was hopin' to take him alive," Fargo said, to no one in particular.

"Your secret's safe with me, mister," McGonigle said.

Fargo vaguely heard the bartender offer him a drink, heard the sound of a glass and a fresh bottle being placed on the bar. He did hear McGonigle comment, "Sweet limpin' Jesus, lookit what we got here."

Fargo looked. Lying at the floor at the base of the bar, a bullet between his eyes, was Hiram Crimp, late of the Armstrong Anvil Company, Pittsburgh, Pennsylvania. His eyes were wide open, but he was as dead as dead ever gets.

"Damn," Fargo said.

He really needed that drink.

Eustace McGonigle went to get the town marshal. A minute or two later, he was back, accompanied by a bear of a man with a bushy black moustache, even bushier black eyebrows, and a generally angry countenance. He was bigger than Fargo by four inches and fifty pounds. A dented tin star was pinned to his vest.

He looked at Pooter McCoy, then at Hiram Crimp. He said to Fargo, "This better be good."

Fargo finished his whiskey. He said, "I think you'll like it."

The marshal motioned to McCoy's body, which was already drawing flies. He said, "You know him, or was he dealing with a hot deck?"

"Both," Fargo said. "Name's Pooter McCoy. He's wanted for some murders back to Salinas. I was sort of hoping this wouldn't happen."

"And this one?" the marshal asked, pointing to Hiram Crimp.

"Wrong saloon in the wrong town on the wrong day."

"It's my hope," the marshal said, "that you got some proof that this Pooter McCoy has a price on his head."

"Wanted poster's in my saddlebag," Fargo said.

"You got a name?" the marshal asked.

"Fargo. Skye Fargo."

The marshal looked thoughtful for a moment. He said, "Fargo, huh? I heard tell of you." He turned to McGonigle and said, "Eustace, you tend to these dead folks. Go fetch Jacob Belinsky. Me and Mr. Skye Fargo is going to retire to my office for a spell. We got some items to talk about." He said to Fargo, "Anytime you're ready."

"Mind if I have another drink first?"

"Go ahead, you'll probably need it," the marshal said. "What's comin' ain't going to be much fun."

The marshal's name was Deke Thornton. He said, "I got two men layin' dead in the saloon over yonder. That don't make me happy, Fargo."

Thornton was sitting at his battered old desk. Fargo took him to be thirty-six, maybe a bit older. His voice was calm, but Fargo knew instinctively that Thornton was a hell storm just waiting to erupt. He'd met dozens like him over the years—leather-tough, hard-working, essentially honest lawmen who didn't cotton to strangers shooting up their towns. Upon entering the jail, Fargo had been relieved of his weapons, and wisely did not protest.

Fargo was sitting in a rickety chair next to the stove. Thornton didn't seem impressed with the yellowing, dog-eared wanted poster for Pooter McCoy, which sat unfolded on his desk. In fact, he didn't seem to care about it one way or the other.

"You would've had six or seven bodies in the saloon over yonder if I hadn't got McCoy first," Fargo said, not bragging, but just stating the facts. "A real animal. Given the chance, he'd have ventilated everyone in the place. Sorry about the drummer. Seemed like a pleasant enough man."

"That don't make him any less deader," Thornton said. "And he got dead in my town. If there's any killing needed done in Flatwater, I tend to it myself and don't need any strangers doin' my job for me. That makes me look bad, and I won't have that."

Fargo said, "Sorry for making you look bad, Thornton, but I got a living to make."

Thornton was up quickly. His eyes were granite. Pointing a beefy finger in Fargo's face, he yelled, "An innocent man is dead, Fargo, and I'm seriously deciding whether to hold you responsible."

This wasn't going well at all. Fargo said, "I didn't kill him."

"He'd still be alive if you'd checked in with me first like you're supposed to," Thornton countered. "But no, you just charged in with no thought for anyone and started trading lead with a man you knew was madder than a shit-house rat. No, Hiram Crimp didn't die by your gun, but you killed him just the same."

Fargo said, with some heat, "I don't see it that way, Marshal. I tracked Pooter McCoy from hell to breakfast, and I know what he was capable of. Poor Mr. Crimp is a small price to pay for what might've been."

"But we'll never know now, will we?" Thornton said. "And in this case, not knowin's what matters. I just might let you cool your heels behind bars until I decide what to do with you."

"There's still the question of the thousand-dollar

bounty on Pooter McCoy," Fargo said. "I'd like to wire the folks in Salinas, let them know the job is done and that they owe me."

"Why should they believe you?" Thornton wanted to know.

"They know me as a man of my word," Fargo said. "Bounty hunting isn't usually in my line. I did this as a favor to some people I know."

"Might take a week for that money to come through," Thornton said. "Don't know if I want you around Flatwater that long. Something tells me you're bad luck, Fargo."

"Yeah," Fargo said. "That happens a lot."

"You got any money?" Thornton asked. "I could always get you for vagrancy if you don't."

"I got enough," Fargo said.

Thornton looked slightly disgusted. He lit a cigar. He said, "All right, Fargo. Against my better judgement, you can get the hell out. Go send your wire. But do it before the sun sets, and find another place to hang your hat till your money arrives."

Fargo wasn't keen on being chased out of any town, much less a one-horse hamlet like Flatwater. He said, "I got a pretty good understanding of the law, Thornton, and unless you got cause to hold me for trial—and you don't—I'm free to come or go as I see fit."

Thornton got red in the face and his moustache twitched. His voice low but rock steady, he said, "Don't you talk to me about the law, you son of a bitch. I don't think I like your attitude, neither. So here's the deal, Skye Fargo. Wait here for your blood money if you want, but if I catch you so much as spitting in the street or breakin' wind in public, I'm gonna cloud up and rain all over you."

"I don't suppose there's any point in asking for my weapons back," Fargo said.

"Not a one," Thornton said, puffing on his cigar. The subject was clearly closed.

Fargo got up to leave. There would be time to argue the matter later. He said, "Is it okay if I get something to eat?"

"Be my guest," Thornton said. "Try Emma's café across the street. The special of the day's chili con carne."

"Okay," Fargo said, making his way to the door. "I won't spit in the street, but when it comes to chili, I ain't making any promises about breaking wind in public."